"Walk me to my car, will you? It's late."

Zack blinked. "Okay."

As she'd hoped, his innate gentlemanliness kicked in and he automatically got to his feet. And then he kissed her.

One moment he was looking down at her with that odd, quirky smile, and the next his lips were on hers. The current that had flowed between them was reestablished just that quickly, and the sound she made that she'd meant to be a protest instead came out like a moan of pleasure.

Reeve had always found him attractive. And perhaps she'd had to spend some time convincing herself back then that giving in to the attraction didn't necessarily have to follow. The fact that he was a man in crisis had made it easy to stay on the proper side of that line.

But now in this moment, with his mouth doing insane things to her nerves, she had no idea where that line was.

Justine Davis
DARK
REUNION

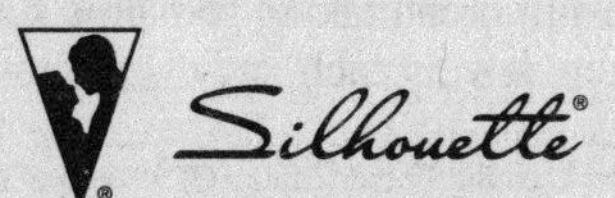

Silhouette
Romantic
SUSPENSE

ISBN-13: 978-0-373-27522-9
ISBN-10: 0-373-27522-6

DARK REUNION

This edition published by arrangement with Harlequin Books S.A.

Visit Silhouette Books at www.eHarlequin.com

Printed in U.S.A.

Books by Justine Davis

Silhouette Romantic Suspense

†*Lover under Cover* #698
†*Leader of the Pack* #728
†*A Man To Trust* #805
†*Gage Butler's Reckoning* #841
†*Badge of Honor* #871
†*Clay Yeager's Redemption* #926
The Return of Luke McGuire #1036
**Just Another Day in Paradise* #1141
The Prince's Wedding #1190
**One of These Nights* #1201
**In His Sights* #1318
**Second-Chance Hero* #1351
**Dark Reunion*

Silhouette Desire

Angel for Hire #680
Upon the Storm #712
Found Father #772
Private Reasons #833
Errant Angel #924
A Whole Lot of Love #1281
**Midnight Seduction* #1557

†Trinity Street West
*Redstone, Incorporated

JUSTINE DAVIS

lives on Puget Sound in Washington. Her interests outside writing are sailing, doing needlework, horseback riding and driving her restored 1967 Corvette roadster—top down, of course.

Justine says that years ago, during her career in law enforcement, a young man she worked with encouraged her to try for a promotion to a position that was at the time occupied only by men. "I succeeded, became wrapped up in my new job, and that man moved away, never, I thought, to be heard from again. Ten years later he appeared out of the woods of Washington State, saying he'd never forgotten me and would I please marry him. With that history, how could I write anything but romance?"

Chapter 1

First one hired, first one fired.

Leave it to her to get that twisted, Reeve Fox thought as she made the turn off the coast highway onto the road leading to the marina. It was supposed to be last one hired, first one fired. Or laid off. Told to resign.

"Whatever," she muttered.

She knew she'd hit bottom when she slipped into useless ponderings like the twisting of clichés. A beautiful, sunny day in Southern California, with people coming great distances to soak up the warmth and enjoy the sand and surf, and here she was, reduced to talking to herself.

Of course, it did help to take her mind off where she was going. For an instant, anyway.

Any of those visitors to the golden shores of this paradise—well, paradise as long as you didn't have to drive in the traffic or plow through the crowds—would no doubt be delighted to have her destination. A summer's day visit aboard a brand-new, luxurious corporate yacht was a treat that few would turn down.

And an afternoon with world-famous international entrepreneur and self-made multi-billionaire Josh Redstone would be a hot ticket for anyone, from those wanting to learn how he'd done it to those simply wishing some of it would rub off on them. Or perhaps hoping he'd part with some of that wealth for their cause, a hope well-founded in Josh's lengthy history of doing just that if you could convince him or move him.

But she was dreading this afternoon. Dreading it because she loved and admired the soft-spoken, gray-eyed man who'd built a dream into an empire and managed to keep it alive and well and prosperous and as tightly knit as a loving family.

Dreading it because Josh was her boss, and she knew he was about to tell her this had to end. Josh was kind and generous and loyal, but he didn't get to where he was by being a pushover. And if he felt he had to, he'd fire her.

She hated the sound of that. Fired from

Redstone. Terminated sounded just as bad. It was very rare that anyone was fired from Redstone. Left by mutual agreement, maybe, but fired? No. Josh's instincts—and his security's background checks—were too thorough. They'd had some bad apples turn up in the past year or so, but they were the very rare exception.

She wondered if Josh would just let her resign. She'd prefer that. And he was a generous man, maybe he would, despite the way she'd failed him. And continued to fail him, holed up in her little house, barely able to function. He'd carried her, paid her for doing nothing for so long now….

She was dead wood, and anyone else would have fired her long ago.

As she took the turn to the marina, she dodged a carload of pointing and gawking tourists in a minivan and pulled in behind an old sedan with a rack full of surfboards on the roof, likely explaining the oxidized state of its once silver paint. The surfers in the sedan looked young, and she wondered if they were old enough even to be aware of the controversy surrounding the building of the marina, that it would destroy the break at one of the best surfing beaches in the county. She'd grown up here in Orange County, and remembered as a child hearing the adults discussing—sometimes arguing—the subject.

Of course, she was older than those surfer kids

were, and about the only thing they had in common was blond hair.

Much older, she thought wearily, and in more ways than one.

While the slightly battered sedan continued on, she turned into the marina parking lot. And her mind went immediately back to the meeting before her.

So much for distraction, she thought wryly.

She turned left at the edge of the marina, heading toward the guest slips that were near the yacht club. When St. John, Josh's ubiquitous and enigmatic right-hand man, had called her to set up this meeting, in his usual laconic way he had said only that it would be afloat. She was never sure if he simply hated to talk or just trusted that anybody who worked at Redstone could figure out the rest.

She wondered just how small the club of ex-Redstone people she was about to join was. Tiny, she guessed; those who were lucky enough to get hired rarely left, at least not permanently. Unless they were stupid enough to break Josh's cardinal rules of integrity, hard work and ethics. Redstone was huge, but somehow Josh, the glue that held it all together, managed to keep that feeling of kinship among his people, fostered by the knowledge that if any of them, no matter how low on the ladder, needed help, the full force of Redstone would be behind them. Like family.

A family, Reeve thought with a sigh as she parked and got out of the car, that was about to divorce her. She looked around. She noted the location of the marina office in case she needed to ask where the boat was. She was peripherally aware of another car pulling into the far end of the same row, saw from the corner of her eye a dark-haired man in a light-blue shirt get out. She glanced at him, thinking he looked familiar, but he was too far away to recognize.

But then she spotted her goal, on a side tie at the far end of the first dock. She'd never seen the boat, hadn't even known this prototype was finished and in the water, but she recognized it immediately. Not because it was flashier or brighter than the other luxury yachts tied up in this large-slipped section of the marina. The opposite, in fact; she recognized it because of the sleek, powerful lines and the subtle Redstone color scheme of slate and red.

The gangway to the dock wasn't particularly steep with the tide in, nor was it slippery, yet Reeve felt as if it were both as she made her way down. She hadn't really realized how much she had come to rely on having the massive force and support of Redstone behind her. Hadn't realized how much she had come to trust Josh Redstone himself.

It's your own fault. You've thrown it away. Even Josh's patience had to run out eventually, and you've let him down for nearly a year.

The litany she'd been running through her head ever since she'd gotten the call from St. John continued in an endless loop as she made her way down the dock. She began to feel as if she were in a tunnel as her field of vision narrowed to nothing but the boat that managed to look racy despite its size and the fact that it was sitting quietly in place.

"Ms. Fox?"

She only realized she'd come to a halt when the voice came from above and snapped her out of whatever zone she'd slipped into. She looked up to see a man who, from the Redstone shirt he wore, was apparently a crew member on the big boat. He was tall, lean and had the tan, slightly weathered face that spoke of life spent outdoors.

"I'm Captain Taggert. Josh is expecting you. Come aboard, please?"

Leave it to Josh to have the captain serve as greeter, she thought. But then again, she realized, it was Josh who made people like the handsome, straight-backed captain here jump to do things before he even had to ask. It was all part of the incredible loyalty and love he inspired in everyone at Redstone, around the world.

She was going to miss it. All of it.

With a vague nautical image of walking the plank in her head, she followed the captain's gesture and walked toward the back—stern, she supposed—of the boat. It was beautiful, she realized on some level of her mind that was able to look at it dispassionately. But then, it was a Redstone, so she would have expected no less.

"Nice boat," she said, feeling pressure to say something.

"Yes," Taggert said. "The man's a brilliant designer. She's set up for work or play. You could host anything from a society wedding to an international conference complete with media connections on this boat."

She nodded, smiling rather wistfully at the pride in his tone. She'd heard back when the keel had been laid that Josh wanted this still-unnamed yacht to be their—meaning any Redstone personnel—escape from the city, which now seemed to stretch unbroken from L.A. to south O.C., when they needed to work or play without interruption.

"Not many would build something like this and then make it available to anybody who works for him," the captain said, the admiration that most who dealt with Josh felt clear in his voice.

The rest of the crew radiated that same pride and admiration she saw as she noted men and women busily going about the tasks of checking, double-checking, and then rechecking yet again every inch of the new and as-yet-untested-by-blue-water vessel.

"The Redstone family," Reeve whispered, aching now that the loss of that family loomed so close. She'd been numb for so long the emotion startled her.

She had the feeling she was about to again see in action the shrewd and sharp mind behind the lazy drawl and unhurried manner, the mind that had built the Redstone empire. The man so many had misjudged as stupid, lazy or naive, much to their later dismay when they realized they'd been out-thought, out-worked and outmaneuvered.

She'd never misjudged him. But she was very much afraid he must feel as if he'd misjudged her about now.

The main salon, as the captain had called it, was also beautiful, with the quiet, understated elegance that typified any Redstone project. In the past, Reeve had wondered if it had been Josh's late, beloved wife who had given him the sense of flawless style, because he himself seemed more of a down-home, comfort-over-style kind of guy.

As he did today, sitting at a banquette with papers strewn across a table made of a beautiful wood burl and polished to a mirror sheen. He didn't look as if he belonged there, tall and lanky in his jeans and simple Redstone T-shirt, his longish dark hair tousled as if he'd just run his hands through it. But this boat, and all the rest of the far-flung Redstone empire, would not exist except for the acumen of the gray-eyed man who turned to look at her now.

"Reeve," he said warmly, unexpected welcome clear in his voice.

"Mr. Redstone," she said, feeling it proper under the circumstances.

The formality stopped him in the act of reaching for her shoulders.

"Mister?" he asked quietly. "I'm still Josh, Reeve."

"I know. You'll never change."

He stepped back, studying her for a moment. "And you have?"

The laziness of his drawl, a combination of all the places he'd drifted through during formative years, didn't fool her. He was on point, and she was the focus.

"Irrevocably, I'm afraid," she said. Suddenly desperate to change the subject, she gestured around her. "It's a beautiful boat. The biggest yet, isn't it?"

For a moment he didn't answer, but finally he let the change of subject happen. "Yes. I don't think we'll go much bigger than this. More than 150 feet and you might as well just build a cruise ship and get it over with."

"Redstone Cruise Lines?" she suggested, managing a smile.

"No, thanks. I've got enough going on with Redstone Resorts. Sometimes I think I should have just stuck with building airplanes."

"The world is glad you didn't," she said, meaning it.

"Not all the world," Josh said wryly, "or you

wouldn't be carrying around that piece of lead that was meant for me."

"Josh," she began, falling back into the old habit of using his first name.

He shook his head, cutting her off, then took her elbow and led her to a cushiony sofa upholstered in a fabric that felt like the richest of suedes. Or perhaps it really was suede, although she doubted it; Josh made the decisions on this kind of thing, and for all his wealth he had a decidedly practical streak.

He sat down at the other end of the sofa, close but not impinging on her space. He studied her again, for a long, silent moment that made her feel beyond awkward.

"I know you don't like to hear it, but I will never forget that you took that bullet for me."

"It was my job."

She grimaced inwardly. The nutcase who four years ago had decided somebody had to do something about the huge entity that was Redstone, and the fact that it functioned so well despite not being run or overseen by the government, had come out of the blue and without warning, but she still felt guilty. It was after the shooting and the revelation that the shooter had a Web site full of psychotic ravings that Redstone Security had widened their scope and begun to monitor the Internet more carefully.

"Really my job was to stop it from being fired in the first place, but failing that...."

"Sounds like Draven," Josh said with a sudden grin.

It did, indeed, sound like the head of the much vaunted Redstone Security team, the tough, unbeatable John Draven. But not uncatchable, she thought, since he'd recently, to the surprise of all of Redstone, gotten married.

It was Josh's grin that did it. She simply could not bear the thought that Josh was keeping her on simply because he felt as if he owed her. Especially since it was, in fact, she who owed him, and she had let him down so badly….

Smothering a sigh, she tried to give him what he deserved from her. "It's all right, I understand. It's not like I gave you much choice."

"Choice?"

She shrugged. "You can't keep paying such an exorbitant salary to someone who hasn't worked in nearly a year. It's time I left, I know that."

"Your salary," Josh said, leaning his six-foot-two length back against the cushions, "is not exorbitant. I want the best, I hire the best, so I pay the best. Simple formula."

It *was* simple, she thought. It was also a big part of what made Redstone what it was. And she supposed he must be right, or Redstone wouldn't be consistently at the top of any Best Places to Work list that was released.

"Yes, but you pay them to *work*," she pointed out.

"I'd prefer you didn't fire me, though. I'd like to resign. Could you have somebody, Sam maybe, pack up my things for me? I don't really want to—"

"Fire you? What are you talking about?"

"You don't owe me anything. You gave me a chance at a great job I loved. You took care of my medical and rehab bills four years ago, and let me ease back into working after the shooting. And now you've done everything possible to get me through this ugliness. It's not your fault or Redstone's that I can't do it."

"I see."

She was afraid he really did, that he somehow saw the dark, yawning hole inside her. She began to talk faster, before that darkness expanded and engulfed her, right here in front of him. "If anything, I owe you. So—"

"Fine. I'm collecting."

His short, blunt words startled her into silence for a moment. "What?" she finally said.

"I'm collecting. I need a personal favor from you. That's why I asked you here."

"Oh."

She felt rather foolish, and didn't know what else to say. She'd been so geared up to deal with what she'd thought she was here for that this unexpected turn left her grasping. And she knew that this was just one more sign that she couldn't return to her job; one didn't survive on the dauntless

Redstone Security team when you couldn't handle a simple unanticipated turn in a conversation.

She also knew that Josh had found the one way around her self-imposed exile; there was no way on earth she could say no to a personal request from him. She could only hope it wasn't anything that would test her tenuous composure.

"Of course," she said, pulling herself together. "What is it?"

"My nephew is missing."

Alarm bells went off in her mind at the very mention of a missing child, but surprise muted them somewhat; she hadn't realized he had a nephew.

As if she'd spoken, he explained. "Rodney is Elizabeth's sister's boy."

"Oh," she said again, sounding so inane she wanted to kick herself. "How old is he?"

"Sixteen. It's not clear-cut, Reeve. There have been some problems recently, some petty crimes, and he has that surly teenager attitude down pat."

"How long has he been gone?"

"Since Friday. He never came home from school."

Today was Monday. The implication was obvious, but Reeve asked anyway; not for nothing had she trained under Draven, who drummed into them all never to assume, even the obvious.

"And he didn't show up at school today?"

Josh nodded. "I need your help, Reeve."

She lapsed into silence, her brief burst of professionalism burned out. She felt a little stunned, both by Josh, who almost never asked for personal help from his staff, and by the fact that he was asking this of her, that she work another case involving a missing child. She wasn't sure the fact that this one was a teenager instead of a toddler made much difference.

"I know he's a punk. But he's Elizabeth's blood," Josh said softly.

Reeve felt a rush of emotion. Everyone at Redstone knew how much Josh had adored his late wife, knew that he'd remained steadfastly alone since her death, no one, apparently, able to measure up to those beloved memories. Even if Josh hadn't stood by her so firmly over these past months, she would have found it nearly impossible to refuse this unexpected request.

"You won't be alone on this, and you'll have all the resources you need," he said. "You've got to try again sometime, Reeve."

He knew what he was doing, Reeve realized. He was giving her the chance to face her demons, to fight this mental fog she'd been living in since she'd arrived too late at the grim, bloody murder scene that had blasted her life to pieces. She'd tried before, had gone back to work three times, only to be unable to focus, to give the job the concentration it required. After the third time, she'd given up fighting to get over it and return for good. Clearly it was going to take more time than she'd hoped.

Maybe forever.

Josh simply waited, watching her. Reeve knew what she was up against. This was a man who negotiated billion-dollar deals the way others bought cups of coffee, a man who persuaded much more powerful people than she. What chance would she have of turning him down, even forgoing what she owed him? And even if she didn't feel she owed him, she still admired and respected the man more than anyone she knew, so how could she—

"There you are," Josh was saying. "Come sit down, Zach."

She blinked, wondering how long she had zoned out this time. She hadn't even realized someone else had come into the room. She turned to look.

She'd half expected someone else on the team, thought perhaps she'd see Rand Singleton or Samantha Gamble, or even Draven himself walking in.

But once again, her expectations were exploded. Her breath shot out of her as if the newcomer had kicked her in the stomach.

Oh, God, she murmured inwardly.

It was the man she'd seen earlier; she recognized the blue shirt. And she couldn't see how she hadn't recognized him even from across the parking lot. How could she not have instantly known that steady jaw, the thick, uncooperative dark hair, the strong, tall frame....

It was the man she'd spent too much time with on her last case. The man whose image was scarred into her memory like only one other.

The man she'd hoped never to see again in this lifetime or any after it.

Zachary Westin. Tied up with the worst memories of her life, memories that had in effect stolen that useful, productive, satisfying life from her. Because his was the case she'd blown. She'd failed, been too slow, too stupid. And because of that the unthinkable had happened.

His six-year-old son was dead.

Chapter 2

He hadn't known.

That was Reeve's first coherent thought after the shock of seeing Zach Westin walk in and sit down in the chair opposite Josh. He hadn't known she would be here.

"Ms. Fox," he murmured, his tone so level Reeve could only guess at the effort it had taken.

He hadn't expected her any more than she had expected him. There was no mistaking the stunned look that had flashed in those incredibly green eyes in the instant before he carefully masked it. Her own feelings were impossibly confused. He had been the first man in a very long time whom she had found herself attracted to, something she'd quashed thoroughly back then. Not only because she'd been a professional on a case; he was married, and that required said quashing in her book.

And a good thing, as it had turned out.

She couldn't look at him. Reeve Fox, once the nerviest, boldest member of Redstone Security this side of John Draven, couldn't meet the gaze of the one man in the world she knew hated her beyond measure.

And rightfully so, she thought, staring down at the gleaming surface of the coffee table in front of her.

She wished she could run. She'd even walk that damned plank she'd imagined if it would get her out of here and away from him.

But she couldn't. She knew she couldn't. No matter how messed up she was, no matter what kind of coward she'd turned into, she couldn't cut and run in front of Josh.

"You said you needed help, Josh," Zach said. "What can we do?"

She marveled anew at the levelness of his tone. He seemed so calm. It didn't seem possible that this was the same devastated man she'd seen a year ago.

Wait until you hear what he wants, she told him silently.

She was sure the last thing Zach Westin would want was to be involved in a missing-child case. Her brow furrowed as Josh repeated the information on his nephew. Why would Zach be here anyway? What would a high-level administrator of Redstone's aviation division have to do with this?

She slid a sideways glance at him. She hadn't seen him since she'd found his son's body in his own garage, a hideously gruesome scene she knew she would take to her grave. It had taken every bit of strength and discipline she'd had to face him then and tell him his little boy was dead, knowing she'd been too slow, too late. She'd only been able to do it by telling herself that however bad it was for her, it was countless times worse for the man who'd lost his only child at the hands of a vicious, cold-blooded pedophile and killer that she should have caught up with in time. That the police hadn't been able to find him either didn't alleviate the guilt she felt over Scott Westin's death.

She found herself trying to shrink down in the sofa, as if she could vanish into the soft cushions.

"—know that this isn't exactly the kind of case the foundation was set up for," Josh was saying, "but it's your area of expertise, not mine, so I have no choice but to ask both of you for your help."

"The Scott Westin Foundation was set up to help any child who needs it, no matter the circumstances," Zach answered. Then, with a wry twist of his mouth that made Josh smile in turn, he added, "Even if the child is related to the boss. I'll get my people to work on this right away."

Reeve wasn't sure what showed in her face, but

Josh's next words were aimed at her. "Zach's running the foundation now."

Reeve blinked. She'd heard about the foundation Josh had set up after Scotty's death, to help anyone who came to them regarding a missing child. But certainly not that Scotty's father was running it. She tried not to think about it at all; if she'd done her job better, the foundation wouldn't exist.

Because Scotty Westin would still be alive.

"You can, of course, utilize Redstone Security if necessary, but you'll work out of the foundation office," Josh was telling her, but Reeve was afloat in her own thoughts and his words barely registered.

She couldn't imagine the kind of strength it had to take for that little boy's father to deal with other children in trouble, some possibly in the hands of someone like the monster who had slaughtered his son, on a daily basis.

He was frowning at her, and Reeve realized she was staring at him.

"Something wrong, Ms. Fox?" he said, reminding her of the way she'd first spoken to Josh. She'd been Reeve, back in those days when they'd been desperately searching, back when there had still been hope.

"I don't understand," she said, meaning it; she knew most people who worked for Josh would do anything for him, but this? "How can you bear to spend your days with people in the same kind of situation that turned your life into a train wreck?"

Not to mention your own life, Reeve, she added to herself. But it was hard to think about the damage done to her when she was in the same room with the man who had suffered the greatest loss a loving father could possibly endure.

"How can I see people in that same kind of situation and not try to save them from that train wreck?"

His answer made her shiver. She'd never felt smaller in her life.

He turned back to Josh. "Have the police been called?"

Josh nodded. "My sister-in-law called them first. But with Rod's prior brushes with trouble at school, and the fact that he's sixteen, nearly seventeen, I doubt he'll get a large share of a plate that's already overloaded."

Zach nodded. "The sheriff's office is already stretched, and they have to prioritize. We're in regular contact with all the agencies in the area, so I know they're working three missings under age ten—two apparent custody grabs, and one that appears to be a genuine kidnapping."

Josh nodded in turn. "Work with them, keep them apprised, use any help they can give you—" He stopped, then gave Zach a rueful smile. "Sorry. I know you know what you're doing. You've worked more than one miracle since you took over the foundation."

Zach shrugged. "I have good people. They're the miracle workers."

Reeve was feeling a bit like roadkill, and at the moment thought she deserved no better.

Josh picked up a manila folder from the coffee table in front of them; Reeve hadn't noticed it until now. He held it out, and Zach reached out and took it.

"Those are the basics about Rod, including the latest photo we have, his school and the make, model and license on his car."

Zach nodded as he scanned the contents. "Does he have a cell phone?"

"He did," Josh said wryly. "In my name. I'm afraid I repossessed it after he ran up a two-thousand-dollar bill in a week."

"Ouch," Zach said, and went back to the folder. After a moment he closed it and nodded again. "We'll find him, Josh. We're clear right now, so he'll be my number-one cause, and I'll do whatever it takes to bring Rod back safely."

Even work with me, Reeve thought, knowing he couldn't be happy about that.

"Thank you," Josh said, and some undertone in his voice told Reeve he wasn't happy about having to call on them. "Rod's having trouble finding his way, but I want him found before he loses any chance he has left."

For the first time in all the years she'd known him, Josh sounded weary. The realization startled

Reeve, and she sharpened her gaze on him. There was a new tiredness in his face, around his eyes. He'd never been an extrovert, smiling and laughing all the time, but today he appeared more grim than his usual laid-back self.

Some instinct kicked back to life in her. There was something else going on here, she thought. More than just a rebellious teenager gone astray.

"Anything else you'd like to tell us?" she asked quietly.

Josh's gaze snapped to her face. His expression changed just slightly, although she couldn't say exactly how. When he finally went on, she had the feeling he'd been going to say something else.

"I'll just ask that, if possible, you keep the media out of it."

"We'll do our best," Zach said briskly. Then he stood up. "We'd better get started. Time is life."

There's a new profundity, Reeve thought as she automatically rose when he did.

Josh smiled at her then. And she realized what she'd seen in his face when she'd asked her only question.

Satisfaction. The look she'd seen before when someone had come around to his way of thinking, or when an opponent did what he'd expected.

Or a colleague.

She'd asked him about that look once. He'd said one was the satisfaction of victory, but the other was the satisfaction of vindication, of being once more proven right in his judgment of people. She wondered what she'd done to bring that on.

As they turned to go, as she walked beside Zach Westin the way she had so many times back in that other life, when there'd been hope, she had the thought that perhaps it wasn't her at all that had put that look on Josh's face. Perhaps it was Zach. She never would have thought the man who had wept in agony over his little son would have been able to put that behind him. Yet apparently he had. And Josh's choice of Zach to run the foundation, no matter how unexpected it was to her, had obviously been a good one.

Which apparently left her as the basket case of the Scott Westin murder.

Reeve's excellent peripheral vision caught him slipping a sideways glance at her as they walked silently back to their cars. Wondering how on earth he was going to stand working beside Reeve Fox again, she guessed.

He stopped before she did at her small, bright-blue coupe. Obviously he remembered the car from last year. While it was still in excellent condition, it hadn't been new then; she didn't feel the need to spend Josh's generous salary on new wheels every year.

"Do you know where the foundation office is?"

"No," she answered.

"It's what used to be the purple place, on Stanford."

"The old house?"

It had become famous for once being painted a vivid purple, as if it were a San Francisco row house. It had looked glaringly out of place, and everybody had known what you meant when you mentioned the purple place.

"Yes. Josh bought it and restored it for us. Including changing the color, thank God. I'll call ahead to arrange a meeting with staff so we can set up a plan of attack for this."

Reeve nodded, but said nothing more, although it felt odd to have somebody else taking charge. Usually, it was Redstone Security who came in and took over whatever was necessary to get the job done. But then, she'd hardly been a part of the Redstone Security team for months now, she had no right to demand the cooperation and respect they had earned around the world.

Besides, it was clear Zach knew what he was doing. He'd learned well in the past year, it seemed. Developed his own way of doing things, and according to Josh, got results. Which was fine with her. As long as he had his own way to go, she could go hers, and, she hoped they wouldn't have to see much of each other in the process. She was certain he'd be happier that way; she had to be a most unpleasant reminder for him.

Although she couldn't quite see how every day

wasn't a reminder for him, not with the work he'd chosen to do. She wondered why he'd accepted the position. She could see why Josh had chosen him; she'd learned last year he was an excellent, well-liked and respected administrator in Redstone Aviation, but for the life of her she couldn't see why he would have accepted this of all jobs.

Just as she couldn't see why his case, of all cases, had so destroyed her. It wasn't as though she hadn't had her own tragedy in life; the death of her parents and the subsequent need to take care of her little sister had turned her life upside down years ago. Perhaps that was the difference, she thought, she'd had too much to do to descend into this well of pain and darkness.

After a moment's hesitation at her silence, he simply nodded and turned away. She watched him for a moment as he walked along the row of parked cars, belonging mostly to carefree people down here for a pleasant day on the water. His thick, dark hair, a bit longer now than it had been a year ago, lifted in the breeze, gleaming. She watched the way he moved, his tall, lean frame seeming somehow coiled, as if it could break loose with an explosion of energy at any second, without warning. Saw his hands flexing, stretching, then curling back almost into fists, then flexing again.

He was many things, was Zach Westin.

Carefree was not one of them.

Chapter 3

With an effort, Zach made himself not look for her in his rearview mirrors as he drove the foundation SUV back to the office.

So, you're not as toughened up as you thought you were, he told himself wryly. One look at her and you lose every bit of progress you've made.

He knew that she wasn't the fragile-looking little blonde he'd first thought her. She'd shown him time and again she was tough, strong and had a stamina that would put many men twice her size to shame. But nothing could change the fact that she was tangled up inextricably with the worst time of his life, a time he prayed to forget and accepted that he wouldn't. Ever.

He pulled in the driveway of the old Tudor-styled mansion in a neighborhood that had once been full of them. It had gradually been taken over by businesses, but the purchaser of these three blocks had had the vision to keep the feel the same, and the row of converted homes was now—at least, now that the purple house was a traditional color—one of the most prestigious business districts in the county. When he'd learned that purchaser was Josh Redstone, Zach hadn't been at all surprised.

He parked at the farthest corner of the small parking area they'd carved out of the courtyard so they didn't have to destroy the lovely garden in front. He assumed Reeve would find her way. He hadn't had to ask if she'd been here; he knew she hadn't. He knew pretty much everything that happened in the building, because his people knew he liked it that way. The shrink he'd seen for a while after Scotty's death had told him it was the need to exercise as much control as he could after the life-changing event over which he'd had no control at all. All he knew was that it was the only way he could continue to function.

As he got out and locked the vehicle, he wondered what Reeve was thinking. She hadn't seemed to want to look at him aboard the boat or after, but he supposed he couldn't blame her. He'd been a raving crazy man for most of the time she'd known him, unable to think of anything except finding Scott, and once they had, once he'd gotten a look at that awful scene in his own garage, he'd completely lost it. He'd been barely human for weeks, maybe even months, so he could hardly hold it against her if she wasn't thrilled about this assignment. There were times, still, that he broke down, times he spent railing against fate, screaming in anger, or just helplessly weeping. But the foundation had given him what he'd needed—a reason to go on.

He heard the sound of wheels slowing, and as he looked up the blue coupe pulled into the driveway. A string of images flashed through his mind, of the times he'd ridden in that car as they followed up on a possible lead to Scotty's whereabouts. She hadn't been happy about it, but he'd insisted.

"You're Redstone," she'd said, "so I'm not going to fight you. Just be clear that I don't think this is a good idea."

Had she been right? Would he have been better off not having ridden that roller coaster of hope and hope dashed? Would he then have been better able to handle that last, unspeakable scene?

He shook his head sharply. He needed to focus. He took all the cases they handled personally, but this was Josh himself. This was family.

He noticed her looking around as they walked into the building. There's a nice, safe, surface topic, he thought.

"They're just finishing up the interior," he explained. "We decided we could live with the chaos for a while, and moved in before they were through just so we could get settled and start work."

The faint smell of new paint lingered, and there were still signs of the recent work in the entry; drop cloths, a collapsed scaffolding, some sealed paint buckets. He made a mental note to verify that the crew was going to be back today to pick up these last remnants of the job.

"They did a nice job," Reeve said as they walked through the building.

"Josh's mandate was to maintain the integrity of the existing design and feel."

"They did. It's charming." She gestured toward the reception area, enclosed with a mahogany railing, and furnished with rich wood shelving and computer desks obviously built carefully to blend with the style of the building. "Even the modern technology doesn't really seem out of place."

"It had to be here. It's crucial to our work."

"I know."

She said it neutrally, but it stung nevertheless. He hadn't realized it until now, but he'd been treating her as if she were a civilian to be taken on a tour of their operation. They did that occasionally, although not as often as the organizations supported by public funding or donations. Bless Josh for that; thanks to the trust he'd set up they didn't have to waste any time or resources on fund-raising. Between the trust and the unsolicited donations that did come in, they were able to run a top-notch operation. Still, he kept the overhead down with few paid staff, but those he had were, in the Redstone tradition, the best.

He cleared his throat. "We're meeting in there," he said, gesturing toward a door at the end of a hallway formed by the waist-high banister on one side and a series of open rooms of the same quality on the other, each with a name by the door. People were busily at work in most of them.

"Better than your average cubicle," she said as they passed.

"That was the idea," he said.

She slowed at the end of the hall, and a glance told him she'd spotted the placard with his name on it outside the door to the end room. It was slightly bigger than the others, but otherwise looked the same.

"No corner office for the boss?" she asked.

He shrugged. "I'd rather have the room to do the work."

He opened the door he'd indicated before, and gestured her inside.

"Ah," she said. "So *this* is the corner office."

"I suppose it was supposed to be."

"But now?"

"It's the war room."

He made no excuse for the terminology. To him, that's what it was. That's what this all was, a war.

A war against one of the worst evils on the planet—those who would do harm to innocent children.

"The others should be here in a couple of minutes," he said. She nodded silently as she began to walk around the room. She looked over the tech corner, where they had three computers and—thanks to Josh and some of his considerable clout in all hemispheres—access to computerized systems worldwide, some that even law enforcement had to jump through hoops to get to.

"That," he said when she paused beside a large piece of equipment, "is a specialty fax, designed to transmit digital photographs that we can also export into a photo-manipulation program."

"To age children?" she asked, referring to the software that could take a photograph of a five-year-old and give a fairly accurate rendition of what that child would look like at any given age.

"Or age them down," he said. "Sometimes all we have is that the child resembles a parent and a photo of that parent. So we reverse the process, back it down in age. And Ian Gamble over in R&D has worked up an amazing bit of software that can take the characteristics of both parents, add in family, home life and environmental factors, and come up with an incredibly accurate image of a child for whom no current photo can be found."

"The resident Redstone genius strikes again," she said with a smile, clearly familiar with the sometimes eccentric inventor. Then he remembered that Ian had married one of the vaunted Redstone Security team, so of course she knew him, probably better than he himself did.

She paused in front of the huge whiteboard that took up half of the outside wall. There were traces of the last case they'd worked still visible in the swirls and swipes of various colors. She looked back over her shoulder at him, a questioning look on her face.

"Just like on TV," he said, his mouth quirking upward at one corner. "We keep a timeline across the top, and then diagram the data we accumulate, and leave it up for anybody to come in and study. Different colors for information from family, official channels, interviews of friends, and highlight any connections in red. It seems to help."

"That makes sense," she said. "I know a couple of investigators who use similar techniques on different kinds of cases, with colors, very effectively."

She smiled. It wasn't the same smile he remembered, that sweet, encouraging smile she'd always used when she was trying to buck him up, keep him going through those dark days. It might look the same at first glance, at least to someone else. Someone who hadn't grown to know that delicate face so well during long, hard hours of high emotion.

He'd also seen that shadow too often to mistake it, seen it in the faces of parents and family—and in his own mirror. There was something eating at her, something that prevented that smile from reaching those huge blue eyes that had once looked at him so gently.

He fought down a shudder brought on by too many emotions to sort out just now.

"Have a seat," he said quickly. "I'll round everybody up."

It was just an excuse to get away from her, he knew that; he'd called ahead and told everyone when to meet him in the war room and they had five minutes before the assigned time. When he got out into the hall and closed the door on her, he let out a breath he hadn't even been aware of holding. When he realized what he was feeling was a sense of escape, he frowned.

He shook off the sensation. Or tried to.

He decided he had enough time to grab a steadying cup of coffee before he had to go back into that room.

She was exhausted. Reeve couldn't believe quite how exhausted she was. She felt as if she'd been working a week straight, full-bore, and all she'd done was meet with Josh and come here. It had taken everything in her just to hold up the facade of normalcy, to ask natural questions that anyone would ask, to pretend this wasn't an agony. And when she had managed it, her words, her voice itself sounded stiff and stilted to her.

At the same time she felt ridiculous. What right did she have to be such a…wuss, she thought, for lack of a better term, when here Zach Westin was, strong, dynamic, dedicated, noble….

The word sounded funny, archaic, even as she thought it. But here he was, facing or ignoring his own past, fighting every day to save others from the hell he himself had suffered through. What other word fit?

She sat at the long table, looking at the others gathered around it. Zach had not taken a seat, but rather stood near the whiteboard now labeled with the name Rodney J. Durbin. J, she'd been told, for Joshua, in honor of his uncle.

Zach had introduced her by name as the others had arrived, saying only that she was from Redstone, helping out because of the connection to Josh.

"Possibilities," Zach said to the group.

"Most obvious, runaway." This came from a man who sat at the far end of the table. He looked to be in his mid-forties, fit, brown hair cut short and with just a touch of gray at his temples. He'd been introduced as Frank Bedford. Zach wrote his contribution on the board. In blue, she noted, beneath the black timeline. Black, she supposed, because it was the only thing they were positive of.

"With Josh as his uncle, isn't kidnapping even more obvious?"

This came from a young woman across from

Reeve. She'd introduced herself to Reeve as Sasha, saying her last name had so many syllables and consonants that she'd wait until they had more time. It made Reeve smile, and now she added this to her assessment; the woman clearly had no problem speaking out and in essence contradicting the older, more experienced man.

To Bedford's credit he didn't even blink. "I'll give you evens on that." He gave Sasha a quick grin as he ceded the point. Zach wrote it down.

"More," Zach said, starting to move around the room as if he were becoming too revved up to be still.

"Amnesia?" This one came in a joking tone from a strikingly handsome man about Sasha's age who had arrived late and pointedly taken the chair right next to the dark-haired young woman.

"As you had about the time for this meeting?" Sasha said sweetly; clearly she wasn't impressed with the joker.

"Put it up there, Russ," Zach said, handing the young man the blue pen. Russ hesitated, looking at Zach as if trying to gauge if he was serious. Evidently he decided he was, or perhaps that it was safer to assume he was, because he got up and added the possibility to the board, looking a bit sheepish.

"Other factors?" Bedford said.

"Maybe that will trigger other possibilities,"

Zach said with a nod. "That he's connected to Redstone, obviously, but what else?"

"He's flunking most of his classes at school," Sasha said, looking down at a notepad in front of her. "And my contact says he's in trouble at school fairly often."

Russ wrote that down in another section of the big whiteboard, having changed, Reeve noticed, to a purple pen. They'd all clearly been through this often enough that everything was automatic.

After he'd finished with Sasha's comments, Russ added one of his own. "He's got a driver's license, as of two months ago," he said as he wrote. "No car registered in his name, but two in his mother's name."

Sasha glanced at the young man's notes. "One of them is the Mustang in the file," she said.

"Go to green," Zach said, startling Reeve until she saw Russ change to a green pen and move to a new section of the board.

"Talk to Mom, obviously," Russ said as he wrote the name *Phyllis Durbin* at the top of the new column.

"I'll take that," Zach said.

"Check at his school," Sasha said. "Officials, teachers, other staff, friends, possible girl—or boy—friends. Russ and I can divvy that up."

"Hangouts," Bedford said. "We need to know where he goes."

It went on, so smoothly and efficiently that

Reeve began to wonder why she was here. These people were obviously very good at this. They had it down to a system that clearly worked very well; the foundation had a very good record at finding missing persons.

"Ms. Fox? Anything to add?"

Her gaze snapped to Zach Westin's face. She cleared her throat. "It seems you have this well in hand. I presume you'll be checking for any prior criminal activities?"

"I've got somebody checking for me already," Bedford said.

"You can take the man away from the cops, but you can't take the cop out of the man," Zach said with a smile at Bedford.

Reeve looked at Bedford more closely. She could see it now, that slightly hardened edge, that world-weariness in the eyes. She should have seen it before, she thought.

He noticed her scrutiny and shrugged. "I got tired of being handcuffed by what society says cops can't do. I wanted to find people, not jump through a million hoops before I could even start looking."

"I understand," she said. "It's why Redstone Security is so effective. We don't have to play by those rules, either."

She heard a low whistle. Then Russ's voice, now tinged with awe. "You're Redstone Security? Seriously?"

I was, she thought, not really sure now how to respond to that. She hadn't been fired, not yet anyway, so she guessed the answer was still yes. But before she could speak, Zach did.

"She was the first Redstone Security agent hired by John Draven," he said. "She'll be a valuable resource before this is over."

A valuable resource, that's me. Like water, or a nice bank account.

She gave herself a mental shake. She was going to have to get out of this rut she'd been living in, full of doubts and second-guessing. This was for Josh, and for him she at least had to try.

She had thought, when she'd first realized Zach was going to be involved, that she'd be able to avoid him through much of the process of finding Rod. She fully intended to, for his sake if nothing else. But now she was beginning to wonder if that would be at all possible. His management style was clearly quite hands-on, and, judging from the reactions of the others, this wasn't just because it was Josh's nephew; he was always in the middle of it, working alongside them. She supposed he had to be, if there were only the four of them plus support staff.

"Okay, that's about all we can do for now here. Everybody know where you're starting? Good. Let's get going. Meeting back here at 6:00 p.m."

"Pizza?" Sasha asked.

"If you must," Zach said, looking up as there was a tap on the door and it opened slightly. The older woman Reeve had seen at the front desk, dressed in unrelieved black, stuck her head in.

"Phone call, Mr. Westin. Mr. Rodriquez. He says it's important."

"Put it through to my office," Zach said, and that quickly he was gone.

"Wonder what's up with that?" Russ said aloud.

"Probably a problem with Brian settling back in," Sasha said. "You know how parents bond with Zach, he's always the one they turn to, no matter how things come out."

So, he got emotionally involved in his work, Reeve thought. He might be pushing harder because of the Redstone connection, but she knew now that every case got his full attention.

"No surprise. Kid went through the wringer," Bedford was saying.

"Brian?" Reeve asked.

Sasha nodded. "A case we wound up two weeks ago. Custodial thing. Alcoholic mother absconded with the ten-year-old son, not because she wanted him but because she wanted dad to pay her to get him back."

"Booze is expensive," Bedford said sourly. He gave Reeve an assessing look. "Redstone Security, huh?"

"Yes." She said it more certainly now. For now, at least, it was still true.

"Quite an outfit. I met your Draven once, a few years back. That's one tough...guy."

She smiled at his last-moment change of terminology. "Yes, he is. He's the best."

"So I've heard. He's got the rep. And it takes the best to get a private force the respect of uniforms all over. Usually we just think of private security as rent-a-cops."

She knew that was true, and almost universal; cops had a tendency to assume that all private-security people were police wannabes, or washouts. But in the years since Josh had set up the Redstone team they had indeed earned the high regard of law enforcement the world over. So high that many of their people were former cops who had been more than glad to leave the strictly regimented job of public servant for the private sector.

"The respect is mutual," she said. "And we know we're less restricted in some areas, so if we can help because of that, we're glad to."

"Heard that, too. One of the reasons when this Redstone chance came up, I went for it."

"Are you glad you did?"

"Beyond glad," Bedford said, fervently enough to assure her of the truth of his words. "I've accomplished more in eight months here than I did in eight years as a detective in L.A. Working for Josh Redstone is incredible. And Zach—Mr. Westin—is the best kind of boss. He's down in the trenches with you, every step. If it goes well, you get the glory, if not, he takes the heat, protects his people."

She wondered if he'd had a police boss who hadn't done that. They were out there, she knew. Another reason she was grateful to be on the Redstone team.

Another reason to get herself out of this rut and try to stay on that team. And, she realized belatedly, she owed it to Draven, too, who'd taken a chance on her as his first hire.

The outer door opened and Zach stuck his head into the room. "Okay, people, let's go. Mrs. Durbin just called Josh with quite a tirade. She needs to see some action."

They scrambled to their feet. Reeve wasn't quite sure what she was supposed to do. As if he sensed her uncertainty, he looked at her and said, a bit more sharply than he'd talked to the others, "With me."

As the missing persons specialist on the Redstone Security team, she was used to being the one running the show, but here it was very clear Zachary Westin was the one in charge.

She couldn't help contrasting his demeanor now with those long, awful days when they'd been searching for his son, and she had been his lifeline, his single thread of hope. Had her failure then created this driven man, or had he always had this potential?

She didn't know. And for the moment, as he impatiently gestured at her to follow him, it didn't matter.

Chapter 4

Zach had never known Elizabeth Redstone, although he'd seen the painting of her in Josh's office. All he knew about her he'd learned from others, and from watching Josh commemorate her too-short life in so many ways. He knew about the Elizabeth Redstone Trust, which supported more charitable causes than he'd ever known existed. He knew about the Elizabeth Redstone cancer wing of the hospital where she had been treated. He was sure there were more memorials that he didn't know about.

He could see a faint resemblance to Elizabeth in Phyllis Durbin. The painting of Elizabeth, even allowing for some artistic flattery, had shown a lovely woman with a good-humored smile and the sparkle of life in her rich, brown eyes. Except for eyes that were paler, this woman had the same coloring, but even though she was the younger sister, she looked much older. Her features seemed…pinched, he thought, unable to think of a better description.

She looked, he told himself, like a woman whose child was missing.

"Please, sit down, Mrs. Durbin," Reeve was saying. "I know the police have been over all this with you, but I'm afraid we need to ask you to go through it again."

"That's all right," she said as she took a seat on the leather sofa in the spacious living room. The entire house was fairly large and nicely furnished. He couldn't help but notice the clutter, shelf after shelf of expensive things, many of them small bits of statuary that were too studiedly cute for his taste. "I'm just glad Josh is going to help find Roddy. I'm so worried."

"Of course you are," Reeve said, her tone soothing as she sat beside the woman and patted her hand. "Any mother would be."

Zach wasn't used to taking a back seat like this, but decided perhaps the woman-to-woman thing would help, and hung back.

"You have children, Ms. Fox?"

"No, I don't. But I raised my little sister from the time she was twelve, and I worried about her as if I were her mother."

Zach noticed the slightest change of expression that flickered across the Durbin woman's face. It was something quick and dark, something Zach couldn't put a name to, but he noted it in his mental file; he firmly believed you couldn't know too much in cases like this.

"And she probably never even says thank you," Mrs. Durbin said. Zach saw the faintest of creases form between Reeve's brows as Mrs. Durbin made a sniffing sort of sound. "People just don't take care of their families the way they should anymore."

Something about her words and tone set Zach off. Before he could stop himself, he said, "So, do you think your son left because he didn't feel taken care of?"

"What?" Her exclamation was sharp. "Of course not! I take the best care of my son."

"Of course you do," Reeve said soothingly. "Now, as any good mother, I'm sure you've spent hours agonizing over where he might be. What possibilities have come to you?"

Slick, Zach thought. She's good. Defused my gaffe and made it impossible for her not to cooperate. He decided things would go better if he just stayed out of it for now, and let Reeve run with it until the woman had a chance to get over her anger at his remark.

"I don't know. I'm so upset and worried I can barely think."

"Have you checked with his friends?"

"I've called the ones I know, yes. No one has seen him."

"Can you give us a list of those names?"

The woman frowned. "I told you, I already—"

"I know," Reeve interrupted smoothly, "this is just to keep us from duplicating your efforts."

"Oh. All right, then."

"He took his car to school Friday?"

"Yes. A new red Mustang. I gave it to him for his sixteenth birthday." She smiled. "He was so excited."

You mean Josh gave it to him, Zach thought. And a sixteen-year-old with a brand new Mustang? I should hope he was excited.

"Can you confirm this is the license number?" Reeve asked, referring to her notes from the info Josh had given them.

"Oh, no, I don't pay attention to those things."

"Do you have the paperwork on it?"

"No, it's in the car, I'm sure."

If Reeve was feeling any irritation at the woman's lack of knowledge, it wasn't showing. But she did change the subject, Zach noticed.

"Any new friends in the picture lately?"

"Not that I'm aware of. But I don't get to see him all that much. I don't get home from work until nearly six." The woman's face took on that pinched look again. "You'd think being related to Josh, I'd be able to stay home and take care of my family…."

He saw Reeve glance around the room, then she flicked him a quick glance. In that second, he was certain she was thinking just what he was, that if she sold off some of this expensive clutter, she could probably afford to stay home until the kid was thirty.

"At least you're able to provide him a lovely home," Reeve said, and Zach knew he'd done the right thing to stay out of it; there was no way he could have said that with a straight face.

He usually found it easy to bond with the parents he dealt with in this work, and he wasn't sure what the problem was here. Perhaps it was that he'd expected someone more like Josh, or more like he imagined Josh's late wife would have been.

Or maybe it was simply Reeve's presence that had changed the dynamic. Did he feel because she was here that he didn't have to bear the brunt of what was always an emotional strain, the first interview with a missing child's parents?

That thought occupied him for some time, and when he finally snapped back to the present, he realized he'd missed more than a little.

"—any strange calls, or strangers hanging around?"

"No, no, nothing like that. Like I told the police, there was nothing out of the ordinary." She sniffed audibly. "All they did was yammer about Rodney getting in a little trouble now and then. He's a high-spirited boy, that's all."

"I don't mean to bring up anything painful, but is Rodney's father in the picture at all?"

The woman's jaw tightened. "Bastard."

She said it so flatly, so quietly, that it seemed more startling than if she'd shouted it.

"Shall we take that as a no?" Zach asked, figuring he'd waited long enough to get involved in this again.

"He tries," Mrs. Durbin said. "He calls, wants to talk to Rod, but the jerk hasn't paid child support in years, so my son wants nothing to do with him."

He doesn't? Zach wondered. Or you don't want him to?

Zach had no idea what his problem was, but when they finally left the Durbin house he was still lecturing himself and trying to figure out why he was so touchy about this one. It had to be because it was Josh, and he wanted to wrap this up successfully and fast for that reason. And he'd do whatever it took to accomplish that.

Even work with Reeve Fox.

"I don't believe it," Reeve said as they pulled out of the Durbin driveway.

Zach gave a sharp little motion that made her think his mind had been a million miles away. When he spoke, it was carefully, as if he were trying to cover his inattention. "Which part?"

"That it's the boy who doesn't want to have anything to do with his father. I think she's just smart enough to say that, knowing she can't withhold visitation because of non-payment of child support."

He slowed the car to a stop at the corner stop sign. "But if it's the child's choice, that's okay."

"It's an out."

Zach sighed. "Exes."

She gave him a quick, sideways glance, just in time to catch the wince that crossed his face, as if he regretted letting that out. She ignored it and spoke quickly; she was, after all, the last person in the world who would want to put any pressure on him.

"I think we can't discard the possibility that the father is involved. That perhaps the boy took off to see him, or even go away with him."

Zach glanced back over his shoulder at the house before making the turn at the corner. "That's quite a cushy nest to fly out of if you don't have to."

"The latest, greatest video game system isn't everything," Reeve said.

Zach's mouth quirked. "You saw that too, huh?"

"It's hard to miss an entertainment system that's built around what has to be a fifty-plus-inch television. Besides, there's the ATM card."

Mrs. Durbin had told them the boy had one on her account, and there was enough in it to take him just about anywhere, although she'd still insisted her beloved son would never leave her voluntarily.

They were back at the main road now, and Zach waited for an opening in the cross traffic. "I wonder how much of all that is courtesy of Josh?"

"Most of it," she said. "Including the house itself."

He looked at her. "You're sure of this?"

"I checked. I wanted to know where things stood before we talked to her."

"What did you do, call Josh himself?"

She shook her head. "St. John."

He blinked, as if the name of Josh's mysterious right-hand man, the enigma who knew all but whom no one knew, was the last thing he'd expected to hear.

"I didn't want to press Josh. You know how he is about his personal generosity staying private. But I knew St. John would know. He always knows. So I called him instead."

"I was under the impression," Zach said wryly as he spotted a break in the traffic and pulled into it, "that St. John's phone lines only went one way."

She laughed. A small one; anything more seemed inappropriate under the circumstances. All of the circumstances. But she felt an odd sort of relief that he was willing to joke with her, keeping to their unspoken promise not to let the past get in their way now.

"A lot of people have that idea," she said. "I think he prefers it that way. He doesn't get bothered much."

"For a long time, I wasn't sure he was real. I

couldn't find anybody who'd actually seen the man. He was just this…voice."

"I can attest that he's real," Reeve said. "I've seen him a couple of times. He has…quite a presence."

She didn't know how else to describe the man who was, by his preference, behind the scenes in any Redstone operation he was involved in. The first time she'd met him, it had been in a room with several people, and yet he had instantly grabbed her attention. Her eyes had shot to him as if he were some well-known rock star, as if some invisible magnetism radiated from him.

It wasn't because of his size or looks—he was just under six foot, and while he was hardly ugly, his attraction wasn't in classical features or smooth handsomeness. And it wasn't simply because she'd known who most of the others were, because she'd honed in on him before she'd even realized who else was there. Nor was it because he was such a mystery, for the same reason.

She supposed it had to be a particularly powerful charisma, although she'd never thought of it as such a tangible thing before. But tangible it was, there was no denying it.

No wonder he stays behind the scenes, she remembered thinking. *Out front, he'd be too much. That Something, whatever it was, would overpower everyone else. And this was no roomful of lightweights.*

"I've always thought he must be the opposite, sort of a quiet, not-really-there kind of guy."

"The reality is quite different, although that's the image he likes to present, I think. But really, think about it, that's more Josh's approach. He sits there, quiet and watchful, so that when he finally strikes, his adversary is left wondering 'Where the hell did that come from?'"

Zach laughed.

Reeve felt an odd combination of heat and cold ripple through her at the sound of his laughter. It was a sensation she'd never felt before, and then she was silently echoing her own spoken words in a very different way.

Where the hell did that come from?

Chapter 5

The peace was holding.

Their agreement to, for Josh's sake, work without reference to the past was holding up.

She, on the other hand, was about to collapse, Reeve thought.

While she knew that after the last year she was no longer in her peak physical condition, she didn't think she'd gotten that bad. It was more that Zach Westin was a machine. He simply never stopped. She knew from her own hours, and the staff's talk about his hours, that he couldn't be getting more than four or five hours of sleep a night.

She had speculated it was because this case

involved Josh's nephew until Bedford, who'd been with the foundation the longest, told her he put in as much time no matter who the missing person was.

"He's driven," the ex-cop said. "This work is his focus, his passion, his life. I don't think he has anything else."

There was a world of experience and knowledge in his eyes, and Reeve took this assessment very seriously. "You make it sound like he's obsessed."

"He is," the man said simply. "But it's not a bad obsession to have."

For everybody but himself, Reeve thought.

She'd grown used to having long hours to herself, her only distractions gardening or a manic round of housecleaning. She'd always been a voracious reader, but even that had fallen prey to her new uncertainty and fears; what if she got caught off guard by something in the story, something that would bring on those horrific memories? She'd retreated even as she'd realized what she was doing, but was unable to help herself.

But now, she was being forced to drag herself out of that protective shell she'd built, just to keep up with Zach Westin. He was relentless, every moment focused on his work. His cell phone was frequently in use, either people calling him to report and ask for orders, or him calling person after person to check on the status. She couldn't imagine what he was like when, as she'd learned often happened, they had several cases going at once.

For now, she thought, and for Josh, she could do this. She'd been well trained, and she could at least act as if nothing was wrong, as if she was still the crack investigator she'd once been. She took a deep breath, and then the first step.

"Would you like me to drive so you can concentrate better on the phone?"

She had thought her voice was even, had been careful not to put any note of criticism in the offer, but his head snapped around as if she had failed at both. "Complaining about my driving?"

She lifted a brow at him. "I wasn't complaining about anything."

He had the grace to look sheepish. "I'm used to working alone," he said after a moment.

"I'm not surprised."

"What's that supposed to mean?"

"Not many could keep up with you."

"I'll be happy to take you home," he said. "I didn't ask for your help."

"No," she agreed. "Nor did I ask to help. But Josh asked."

That took the heat out of the mad he was building. She wasn't sure what—or who—he was mad about, but she didn't want to deal with it.

"I was simply offering to drive. You're working

with your people, you have a system, a rhythm, which might be better served if you didn't have to do both."

"I can do both."

Stubborn, she thought in mild exasperation, although she knew that wasn't the sole explanation. It didn't take a rocket scientist to figure out what was driving him. Over the years she'd seen people handle grief in different ways. Or not handle it at all. She wasn't sure if Zach was channeling his into this work, or using the work as a means of denial, but there was no doubt in her mind that it was his grief that was fueling the passion for this work. Just as there was no doubt in her mind that either way was a path to breakdown or burnout unless he got a grip on it.

Listen to you, the expert who can't even get her own act together, she muttered inwardly. The knowledge allowed her to gather her patience before she spoke again.

"I'm sure you can. I'm sure you can work twenty-four-seven, three sixty-five, keep every one of your staff doing the same, and do what's probably a full-time job in itself, managing the foundation on top of that. What you can't do—"

She stopped herself when she realized what she'd been about to say.

"Is drive and talk at the same time?" he suggested, his mouth twisted into a wry grimace. "What?" he prodded when she didn't answer.

"Is save them all," she said softly. "And even if you could, it wouldn't bring—"

He swore harshly as he yanked the wheel of the car, pulling so sharply to the side of the road that she didn't finish the sentence she realized she should never have begun anyway.

"Don't," he ordered sharply. "Do not go there."

He got out of the car and walked to her side, and yanked the door open as sharply as he'd turned the wheel.

"You want to drive, drive. Just shut up while you do it."

She didn't offer a retort, or any kind of defense. It had been a stupid thing to say, and she of all people should have known that and kept her mouth shut. She was, she thought as she got out and walked to the driver's side, lucky he hadn't taken the opportunity to remind her whose fault it was that they were both here, doing this, at all.

Because what she'd started to say to him applied to her as well, perhaps even more strongly. No matter what she said, what she did, or how hard she worked, there was one thing she couldn't do.

She couldn't bring little Scotty Westin back.

Zach couldn't remember the last time he'd lost his temper. At least, not with a person. He lost his temper all the time with cases that didn't go well, but he confined expressing his frustration to inanimate objects or the case itself.

When he misdialed three calls in a row, he sourly told himself it was a good thing he didn't lose it often, if this was the result.

As he sat there with his uncooperative phone in hand, an unfamiliar ring tone made him do a double take, checking to be sure his phone hadn't mutated somehow. But when Reeve dug into her pocket and pulled her own out, he relaxed. She glanced at the outside screen, then pulled over to the side of the road and flipped the little phone open.

"Fox."

As she listened to the caller attentively Zach could hear that it was a male voice.

Very attentively, he thought. Boyfriend? he wondered. She hadn't been married last year, a fact that had surprised him. She was beautiful and smart and kind, and he couldn't believe some man hadn't grabbed her and held on. She still didn't wear a ring, although that wasn't quite the reliable signal it had once been.

"Yes, sir," she said. "I'll pass it along, with your recommendations."

So much for the boyfriend theory. Josh, perhaps?

"Fine. This is for Josh, so I'll get through."

His brow furrowed at her words as the possibility of the head of Redstone being the caller vanished. Why wouldn't she get through?

"Your training is like riding a bike, you don't forget. Wobble in the beginning maybe, but you don't forget." There was a pause before she said, "I don't know yet. I just don't know. I'm sorry."

When she hung up a few seconds later, he gave her a questioning look. "Problem?"

"No. My boss."

"The infamous Draven?"

She nodded. And smiled, although it appeared rather half-hearted. "He's worried about me. He never would have admitted that before, but Grace has warmed him up a bit. Never thought that was possible."

"She's something," he said. "And Redstone throws quite a wedding."

"Yes."

She was avoiding his eyes, which was different enough that it caught his attention. "You didn't go to Draven's."

"No." She closed her eyes for a moment. "I was…on an extended leave."

His gaze narrowed. "Were you injured?"

"No."

He was even more puzzled now. If she wasn't hurt, why had she been on leave? Or was she still?

"Should you even be here?"

"A question I've been asking myself," she muttered.

She sounded, he realized, bitter. In all the time

he'd spent with her, and it had been nearly twenty-four hours a day for the three weeks Scotty had been missing, she'd never sounded like that.

Extended, he thought. She'd said extended. "How long?" he asked.

She blinked. "What?"

"How long have you been on leave?"

"A while."

He studied her for a moment before saying quietly, "You never lied to me. All that hell, and you never lied. Why now?"

"This is my personal business," she said, her voice taking on an edge.

He drew back slightly. Realized he'd crossed a line, and wondering why it had seemed so important to him.

"I'm sorry. You're right. It's none of my business."

She gave him a startled glance, as if she hadn't expected him to give up so easily.

"I didn't mean it…so harshly."

"Doesn't matter. Let's move on."

After a moment she looked away. He saw her take a deep breath. Then she pulled the car back out onto the road. It wasn't until they pulled up at a red light that he remembered the beginning of her conversation.

"Did Draven call about this case?"

"Yes. He got the info on the bank accounts the

ATM card is linked to, so we can put a watch on them."

He blinked. "That was fast. We usually have to jump through a lot of hoops to get that. Or get it from the police."

"It helps that Josh is on the board and owns better than half the bank. Plus, he opened the accounts and makes the deposits, so he technically can release the information. And between the checking and savings, there's a healthy five figure balance."

"Great. So the kid's got access to plenty of money. Maybe Josh should freeze the accounts."

"Draven and Josh discussed that. But they put a flag on the accounts instead, to be notified if and when either is accessed, and from what branch."

"That will help."

"He's also got a good police contact, somebody he's worked with before. Word is they've put out a description, and they're doing the basics, but until more time passes or there's a ransom demand, Rod is only one of many teenagers who have either run away or just plain forgotten to call."

Zach nodded; he'd expected that. There just wasn't the manpower or the time to devote to every almost-adult kid that went astray.

"And Josh doesn't want any special treatment or attention, I'm sure," he said.

"No. Not only because it's not his way, but because the more attention they give the case because of who he is, the more crackpots that creep out from under their rocks."

He nodded. "When you're one of the most famous, rich, and most notoriously generous people in the world, you might as well be walking around with a target on your back."

"I asked him once," Reeve said, remembering, "if he worried about extortion or that kind of thing. He said when you had a family the size of Redstone, you had to worry."

"I know. He went to the wall for Scotty."

She winced.

He knew he'd seen it, although the expression vanished almost as quickly as it had appeared. An idea came to him, one that hardly seemed possible given the competent, tough investigator he'd come to know in those horrible days. But still he wondered. He couldn't ask, she'd made it clear it was not a topic for discussion. At least, not with him. But he'd find out. Somehow.

Even if he had to call the mighty Draven or the mysterious St. John himself.

He didn't know.

Reeve was surprised at first, but after she thought about it a little, she realized she shouldn't have been. Why on earth would he know she'd been virtually crippled since the day she'd found his son's brutalized body? It wasn't as if he would have cared. Why should he? Nothing, absolutely nothing could be worse than what he himself had gone through. Why would he even spare the slightest of thoughts for the woman who'd been too late, who hadn't been able to do her job and save him from that agony?

He couldn't have had the energy to do anything but get through each day, not after what had happened. It was amazing he was functioning at all, let alone at the pace he was keeping.

She didn't know what he was running on. And she didn't want to know what would happen when he hit the wall, as he inevitably would. No one could keep going like this indefinitely. Not in this kind of work, heart-crushing work that would eat away at anyone, but most especially someone who had lived through his nightmare.

She was sure it was why he was so good at it, why the foundation had developed its amazing reputation so quickly. But at what cost to him? How could he keep doing this, day after day? He'd told her he couldn't not do it, but surely he had to know there would be a price?

They had just arrived back at the foundation office to add what they'd learned from Rod's mother to the information board when her cell rang again. She recognized the number as being from Redstone Headquarters, but not the number itself.

"Fox," she answered.

"It's Josh," the male voice said, as if anybody who worked for him wouldn't immediately recognize the soft drawl.

"Yes, sir," she said, trying quickly to gather facts for some kind of a report. "We've just come from Mrs. Durbin's—"

"I didn't call for a progress report, Reeve. At least, not on that."

"Oh."

It took her a moment to realize what he meant. Understandable, she thought; how many billionaire bosses would bother to call to check on an employee? Not that she didn't know he did it, she'd heard the stories, she'd just never expected it to be her. She glanced around, and found an empty office to dart into; this was not a conversation she wanted to have in a public place.

"I know you'd rather not be doing this. And that another missing-person case is the last thing you wanted."

"No, it's fine. I don't mind."

"Is that because you really don't, or because it's me and you think you can't?"

Reeve grimaced, glad he wasn't here in person to see her face. "A little of both?" she suggested wryly.

He chuckled, and it was a warm sound that erased the grimace and made her smile. "I'm glad you've hung onto your sense of humor. Sometimes that's the only thing that gets you through."

"It's either laugh or cry." Or throw up, she added silently, remembering waking up from the recurring nightmares of lakes of blood and a dead child.

"Sometimes all of those at once," Josh said, his tone so gentle she wondered if he'd somehow heard the shudder that went through her. "I thank you for taking this on, Reeve."

"Not necessary," she said.

"You could have said no."

She grimaced again. "I like working for Redstone."

There was a long pause before Josh said quietly, "Did you have some idea you wouldn't be, even if you did say no? I thought we resolved this, Reeve."

"But...I still don't know if I can do it. Come back."

"To Security, you mean?"

"Yes."

"Then we'll find you something else."

This had never occurred to her. "Something else?"

"Whatever you want to do. You're Redstone, Reeve. We don't toss aside family."

After she'd hung up, she sank down into the desk chair she'd been standing beside, staring at the cell phone in her hand.

She'd underestimated him. Just as so many others had, over the years. Josh Redstone was indeed one of a kind.

Her mind went back to what she'd been thinking about Zach. About the price to be paid for the passion and energy and soul he poured into this work.

And wouldn't you pay any price to help Josh?

There was only one answer to that. This was to help Josh, so what did the cost matter? Perhaps that's what kept Zach going at such a pace. Perhaps he'd do anything to make sure Josh didn't have to go through any version of the hell he'd survived.

And so should she. It was time to get her act together. She could do that, for at least as long as this took.

And after?

That, she'd decide when the time came. It didn't weigh nearly as heavily on her now that Josh had laid the Redstone world at her feet.

Yes, she would pay any price to help that man.

Starting now.

Chapter 6

"Have you seen Zach?"

Reeve looked up to see Sasha entering the room she'd retreated to to take the phone call from Josh. She realized it must be the woman's working space when she put a stack of papers down on the desk and opened the drawer for a pen.

"Sorry," she said. "I needed to take a phone call."

Sasha brushed off the explanation. "No problem. If we want privacy, we close the door."

Reeve smiled at her, then answered the original question. "I haven't seen Zach in the last twenty minutes or so."

"Lord knows where he is then. That man can cover a lot of ground in twenty minutes."

"Does he always go at this pace?"

"Well, he might be pushing a bit harder because this is Mr. Redstone, but pretty much, yeah."

"Does he ever take a break?"

"Not since I've been here. Oh, he has to take off now and then to deal with his ex, but other than that...."

"His ex...?" He'd divorced?

"Yeah. Deborah." Sasha shook her head wonderingly. "He's so patient with her. She's never been the same since...you know."

Reeve remembered the woman, although she hadn't dealt with her much while they'd been searching for Scotty. She hadn't been too functional, and Reeve remembered her mostly seesawing between sobbing heartbreakingly and yelling furiously. It had been exhausting for all concerned. Fortunately, the detective who had worked the case had a knack for calming people down, so he'd taken over handling Deborah while Reeve dealt with Zach.

"I didn't realize they'd split."

"Odds were on it," Sasha said.

Reeve knew that, knew the lopsided statistics on the marriages of parents of murdered children. She'd heard Zach and his wife fighting a couple of times, but had chalked it up to the fact that Zach was expending all his energy and patience on the search for his son and had none left for his frantic wife.

She even remembered urging him to spend some

time with Deborah, comforting her. She thought he'd tried, but obviously it hadn't been enough. Or Deborah had needed more than he had left to give.

She snapped back to the present when she realized Sasha was studying her intently.

"It was you, wasn't it? You're the one who worked on his son's kidnapping?"

She'd wondered if he'd told them. Obviously not. With an effort, she answered levelly. "Yes."

She waited for the inevitable, for the questions, or the astonishment that Zach would even allow her in the building. It didn't come.

"That must have been awful," was all Sasha said.

"It was."

"It's why he's so dedicated," Sasha said. "And he gets even more that way after they have a blowup."

"They have blowups? Still?"

"Some ballistic ones. At least on her part. Zach tends to get quiet. He just takes it."

Sasha looked suddenly embarrassed, as if she'd betrayed Zach by talking about his personal life.

"Enough of that," Reeve said briskly, before Sasha could feel any worse. "I've got some databases to check."

She walked back toward the room that housed the bank of computers and found Zach, a cup full of coffee that looked suspiciously thick in his hand, staring at the whiteboard now covered with names, dates, places and miscellaneous bits of information people had uncovered thus far. Staring, but not really focused on anything; his gaze had that distant look that told her his mind was somewhere else.

She didn't think she wanted to go to wherever that was, so she turned to leave. Quietly, she thought. But he spoke anyway.

"Avoiding me?"

She stopped. Looked back at him. "Trying not to disturb you. Different beast altogether."

He looked at her then, and she saw the shadows in his eyes retreat. For now, at least.

"Sorry I snapped at you before."

"Don't be. I shouldn't have said what I said."

"Why?" He let out a long, compressed breath. "It's probably true."

She didn't quite know what to say to that, so said nothing. He took a long sip of the coffee, grimaced as if it were indeed as strong as it appeared, then set the mug down on the big table. He stared down at it, as if the answers were all in the dark-brown liquid.

"I just heard about you and Deborah. The divorce. I'm sorry."

His head snapped up. He looked at her, and she had a sudden flash of memory, of the first time he'd ever turned those penetrating, laser-sharp green eyes on her. They were startling anyway, beneath the thick shock of dark hair, but the intensity of them took her aback now as it had then.

"So am I," he finally said as whatever had fired that look began to fade.

"It's not a shock, given the statistics—"

"It's always a shock if it's you," he said.

Reeve smothered a sigh. She was usually pretty good with people, but it seemed everything she said to this man was wrong. Perhaps she'd been too optimistic in thinking they could work together.

Zach turned away, and walked over to the single window in the room. He stared out for a long, silent moment.

"I shouldn't have been surprised," he said finally. "By any of it. Deborah filed for divorce two weeks after we found him. She wanted me to fix it, and I couldn't. So she left."

"Fix…what?" Reeve asked, her tone cautious.

"Scott. It was my fault, so it was my job to fix it."

Reeve went very still. "Your fault? Your son's death?"

"I was his father."

"Why does that make you responsible?"

"She had a point. It took me a long time to get past it."

"What point?"

"I was supposed to protect him. I didn't, not well enough."

"And I was supposed to find him." It broke from her involuntarily. "If anybody's to blame, I am."

Zach turned so suddenly Reeve nearly took a

step back, although she was still across the room from him.

"You? Why would you be to blame?"

It came out in a rush that she couldn't even slow down, let alone stop. "It was my job, you and Deborah and Josh and Draven all trusted me to find him in time. I didn't."

He walked toward her. Only when he stopped a yard away did she let out the breath she hadn't realized she'd been holding.

"I have never," he said quietly, "seen anyone work harder than you did to find my son. You couldn't have done more if he'd been yours. It's not your fault we didn't get there in time."

"Zach—"

He held up a hand and she fell silent. "There is one person, and one person only, who is to blame for Scotty's death. And that's the sick, twisted, perverted psycho who murdered him."

Reeve managed not to gape at him, but barely. Finally she had to lower her gaze; it was simply too much to look at his face. All this time she'd assumed he despised her, that he blamed her for his loss. And she'd accepted the blame he'd now made clear was imagined, because….

Because you blamed yourself.

That a big part of the torment she'd endured over the past months apparently had been self-inflicted was not a realization she could quickly absorb.

"Are you telling me you've been blaming yourself all this time?"

"It was my job," she repeated. Then, in a voice she barely recognized as her own, she whispered, "He was *like* my own. I got to know him so well, from you, when you would talk about him. His personality, his cleverness, his big heart...he became alive to me as no other case before had. And I wanted to find him, save him, more than I ever had anyone before. For you, but not just for you...for me, too."

She hadn't realized any of this until this moment. Hadn't realized that the child she'd hunted for so desperately had become much more than just a job to her during those long, desperate hours.

Slowly, almost afraid of what she might see, she finally looked up at him. There was an expression on his face she couldn't name, some combination of remembered pain and surprise and empathy that made her heart feel squeezed in her chest.

"That's why you've been off work, isn't it?" he asked softly. "You haven't been back since...since Scotty, have you?"

Slowly, unwillingly, she shook her head.

He lifted a hand, reached out and cupped her cheek. "It wasn't your fault," he repeated. "And I'm sorry you've been feeling this way for so long. But that you were...honors my son. Thank you."

He left abruptly, swiftly, as if escaping. Left her

standing there, stunned, emotions tumbling inside her, so many she couldn't hold onto any one of them.

She had some serious rethinking to do.

"I didn't even know Claire had a sister," the girl with the pierced eyebrow said, eyeing Reeve suspiciously.

Reeve knew she had to step carefully here. With her undercover experience, and given that a woman would be less likely to be perceived as any kind of a threat or draw too much attention, she'd been the one to go to Rod's high school. She'd picked the cover carefully, the older sister of a student who had transferred when her family had moved, and who shared her own blonde, blue-eyed looks.

She'd been able to find out names of a couple of the girl's friends, but Madison was the first one she'd been able to find. She just had to hope they weren't still in constant contact.

"Yeah. I didn't see her much when she was going here, since I was away at college." Reeve's mouth quirked. "Guess it's my fault she had to move. The parents didn't trust me away from home alone."

"Parents are such losers," the girl said with a commiserating groan.

"Anyway, Claire asked me to see if I could find out if her old boyfriend was still around."

"You mean Garth?"

Reeve frowned. "No. Must have been after him. Or before. I think I lost track." She made a face she thought the girl would understand. "Boyfriend trouble of my own. They can be such idiots."

"Tell me about it. Why didn't she just e-mail me?"

"I don't know. Do you?"

The girl frowned. "Probably because I promised to e-mail her every day, but after a couple of weeks I got busy and didn't."

"She's not mad or anything. Really."

Madison's expression lightened. "Good. And really, she didn't e-mail me back much, either."

"Life's crazed," Reeve said. "Anyway, this guy's name is Rod. Rod...Durbin, I think."

She was rewarded with a smile, but also got a puzzled look. "I know Rod, but he and Claire never hooked up. In fact, she didn't like him much. Good thing, too, I heard the cops were here looking for him."

"Really? That doesn't sound like somebody Claire would like."

"No. She thought he was a snob. Always talking about how he was related to some rich guy who was going to leave him everything. Like we were all supposed to be nice to him and like him because he might have a Ferrari some day."

Charming, Reeve thought. "Talk about idiots," she said, earning a grin this time. "I wonder why she wanted to know about him, then," she went on, as if she were as puzzled as Madison. "Did the cops find him?"

"Not that I heard. And I haven't seen him today at all. And believe me, if he's around, you can't help knowing it."

Reeve laughed. "Well, I'm going to have to chew out my little sister. I think she was setting me up. Unless—I wonder if maybe he did something to her, and she wants to find him to do something back?"

The girl's brows rose. "You mean like payback or something?"

"Maybe that's why the cops were looking for him. He ever do that kind of thing, like play tricks on people?"

"Well, yeah, stupid stuff, like M-80s in lockers, and harassing freshmen for money, but I don't think he ever tried anything on Claire."

"I hope not," she said. "Maybe I should talk to the little boy and find out, though. Any idea where he hangs out, or who with?"

"There's an arcade at the mall. He's kind of a geek that way. Cuts class to go there, why, I don't know, since he's supposedly got this hot gaming computer at home."

Maybe home isn't so much fun, either, Reeve thought, remembering the interview with the boy's mother.

"Friends?" she asked.

"He mostly hangs with a couple of other loser-types, Chuck Barker and Patrick something. They go with him to the arcade, but I think only because he pays."

"Thanks, Madison."

"Sure." A bell ringing sounded the end of the lunch break and their conversation. "Tell Claire hi for me. And that she's lucky to be out of here."

Most teenagers probably felt that way, Reeve thought as she scribbled down the names after Madison had gone. Wherever they lived, someplace else had to be better.

Sometimes anyplace else.

He should just program her cell number into his phone.

Or rather, reprogram it.

It was the same number. He was certain of that. Just as he was certain of how many times he had sat staring at his phone a year ago, willing himself not to call her for the second time in an hour, to ask if there was any news.

He hadn't deleted the number for months after. She'd been his anchor in those dark days, the only one who seemed to be able to steady him, the one who gave him hope. He'd called her when he'd had an idea, or when he'd run out of them, and she always had managed to keep him from giving up.

But afterward, she'd given up herself. Or on herself.

He was still a little stunned that she'd blamed herself for Scotty's death. He supposed a certain amount of that was to be expected in someone dedicated to their work, but that it had put her out of commission for nearly a year made him feel…

He wasn't sure what it made him feel. There were too many emotions involved in his reaction to that, too much to sort out. Now, at least.

He dialed the number that was still etched into his memory.

"Fox."

He resisted the temptation to respond "Westin," to keep it professional. In his mind, they'd passed professional when he'd broken down the night they'd found his son, and she'd been the one to hold and comfort him while he wept like a baby.

"It's Zach," he said instead. "Any luck at the school?"

He listened while she gave him what she'd found out.

"Rod's two friends weren't at the arcade, although they'd been there earlier. When they left they were talking about getting something to eat, and the guy who works at the arcade said Chuck has the hots for some girl who works in the food court. I'm headed there now," she finished.

"I'll meet you there. Bedford found out a couple of things."

Better the food court, he thought as he hung up and made the left turn that would take him to the mall, than the arcade. That place brought back too many hard memories. Scotty had loved the children's room, with the games aimed at younger kids. There had been a game based on his favorite cartoon show, and he would gladly play it for hours if allowed. He wasn't, which had been a problem until Zach had bought the boy a watch with a timer, and made sure he knew going in that when it went off, game time was over.

He fought down the rising pain. He wasn't foolish enough to think he'd ever get over it, but he hoped some day it wouldn't stab quite as deeply or as often. Some day.

He focused on parking and locking the car near the food-court entrance, then headed for the doors. On this mid-week day, most of the occupants of the large, circular area ringed by various fast-food enterprises were women with children in tow, many literally, in strollers. The decibel level was correspondingly high, and he tried to tune it out as he scanned the area.

His breath caught in his throat as his gaze snagged on a petite, beautiful but almost fragile-looking blonde. It was a split second later that he realized his breath had caught because it was Reeve.

He'd never seen her quite this way, at a distance, amid a crowd. She stood out like golden light on a gray sea, and drew him toward her so strongly he wondered if he could have stopped if he wanted to.

Only then did he spot who she was talking to, and his brow furrowed. The boys, one dark, one sandy-blond, looked young, but still they were taller than her, and there were two of them. As he got closer he realized they were flirting with her. He couldn't fault their taste, but as the dark-haired one moved in closer to Reeve, he felt himself tense, and instinctively took a step toward her.

With that almost preternatural awareness that had always startled him before, she glanced in his direction. With a barely perceptible shake of her head she warned him off and went back to chatting with the two teenagers.

He slowed, not liking the idea of leaving her alone to deal with them. But she was the pro, she knew what she was doing. He remembered asking her before, in one of those exhausted moments of searching for distraction, if she had a black belt in some martial art. She'd smiled, and told him she had something even better, training by Draven.

Having now met the man, he had a greater appreciation for what she'd meant. And he stopped about ten feet away, pretending to study the menu of a stall offering various forms of Chinese take-out as he listened. Apparently she hadn't been there long.

"—business is it of yours?"

"I work for his uncle."

Eyebrows shot up on both teenagers. "That Redstone guy? The bazillionaire?"

"Yes. So, have you seen Rod?"

"Not for a couple of days. He was supposed to meet us at the arcade at two-thirty Friday," the dark-haired one said, "but he didn't show."

He seemed to cast a glance at the girl behind the counter at the pretzel stand, and Zach wondered if that was the one Reeve had mentioned one of the kids had the hots for, and if he was trying to use Reeve to make her jealous. If so, it seemed to be working; the girl was watching them not too surreptitiously.

"Yeah, and I wanted to play that new game, too," the other boy groused.

So why didn't you just go ahead and play? Zach wondered silently. *Counting on Rod to pay your way?*

He muttered that he hadn't decided yet when the girl behind the counter asked if he was ready to order.

"Maybe he had a date?" Reeve said, smiling at the boy.

The sandy-haired teen snorted inelegantly. "Yeah, right."

"Rod doesn't date," his friend said. "He's pissed at girls."

"All girls?" Reeve asked.

The dark-haired one smiled back at her in a way that made Zach go tense. "Well, he hasn't met you yet, has he?"

"I think I'm a bit old for him."

"Hey, older woman, younger man, it's cool now."

"There is that," she said, as if seriously considering it.

Zach waved the girl off again, thinking that in a moment he was going to have to order something just to keep those kids from noticing him. He actually glanced at the menu, just in case.

"But why is Rod so angry with half the world's population?"

It seemed to take the boy a moment to get it. "Oh. He thinks they only pay attention to him because of his money."

"How do they know he has money?"

"Uh...he tells them?"

"Besides," put in the quieter one, "he drives that sweet car. It's pretty obvious."

At sixteen, Zach thought, he'd still been walking to school, except when his mom didn't have to go to her second job and could drop him off.

"Seen the car around lately?" Reeve asked.

"Nah. He won't let anybody else drive it, so if we'd seen it, we would have seen him."

Reeve smiled at this example of male teenage logic. "Guess so. Well, if you see him, tell him to call his uncle. It's about that trip to Australia."

"Australia!" the boys exclaimed in unison.

"Thanks, guys," she said casually, and waved at them as she turned and walked away. They gaped after her, and Zach had the feeling it was caused as much by Reeve herself as the mention of a trip to Australia.

And as he watched her head toward the mall doors he had the feeling the look on his face was probably painfully similar to that on the faces of the two teenage boys.

Chapter 7

Feeling a bit guilty, Zach quickly ordered a couple of egg rolls from the patient girl behind the counter. She handed them to him just as Reeve reached the doors. He thanked the girl, tipped her the change, and headed after Reeve. She wasn't in sight by the time he got outside, and he scanned the parking lot.

He found her waiting by his car.

"You heard most of that, I assume?"

He nodded. "Nice trick, that Australia bit."

She smiled. "I figured that'd bring on some sort of contact, if they can reach him."

"And probably a demand that he take them with him," Zach said wryly.

"You got that feeling too? That his friends are literally in it for the money?"

He nodded. "The only question is, did he buy them, or did they smell money and start circling?"

"End result is probably the same," Reeve said with a sad shake of her head. "Poor Rod."

Zach nodded, then asked, "You parked back by the arcade?"

"As far from here as you can get, of course."

"Get in, then. I'll drive you back to your car and I'll fill you in on the way."

She hesitated for a moment. "Are you sure you want to go anywhere near the arcade?"

His earlier memories flooded his mind again. She knew about Scotty's affinity for the arcade, of course; they'd checked it countless times in the hopes his son might somehow turn up there.

"I'm sure I don't," he said, his voice sounding a little tight even to himself. "But there's no place I can go that doesn't make me think of Scott. Even places he'd never been."

She studied him for a long moment before saying quietly, "And that's really it, isn't it? You carry it with you, so there's no escape."

Her words described it so exactly that he almost winced. "Exactly," he said.

She'd always seemed to understand, he thought, as they got into his car. He'd even asked her once how she knew how it felt. Had asked her who she'd lost.

Everyone, she'd said then.

The look in her eyes had told him she'd meant it literally. He hadn't thought he'd be able to bear the story of such loss, not then. He'd only heard the details later, of the crash that had killed everyone except her little sister.

He wasn't sure he could deal with it now, either, so he didn't bring it up. But he remembered.

"You were going to tell me what Bedford found out?"

He snapped back to the present. "Yeah. He ran the license plate on the Mustang, so we've got the VIN number now."

He made the turn at the south end of the mall, where the arcade was. Then he dug into his pocket and handed her the slip of paper he'd written it down on. She pulled out her PDA and added it to the electronic file she was keeping.

"He also found out Rod was pricing a very expensive car stereo system last week. Guess the one in the Mustang wasn't loud enough. Or not enough bass," he added with a grimace.

"Hey, it's a rite of passage. When you're a kid, you want the world to know what music you're listening to, so they know you're cool."

"And when you grow up?"

"Then you're just who you are and you don't care what they think of you." He saw her mouth tighten at one corner. "That's excluding sociopaths, of course."

Zach felt the stab, as usual, but fought it down.

"Sorry," she said quickly, although he didn't think he'd betrayed anything. "I didn't mean to—"

She stopped when he shook his head. "It doesn't take someone mentioning it to remind me that it was a sociopath who murdered Scotty. It's as you said, you carry it around with you all the time."

"Yes. It would be."

He spotted her car and turned down that aisle. The space one over was open, so he took it. He put the car in Park and then looked over at her. She was sitting quietly, her eyes lowered, staring at the PDA in her hand. But he had a feeling she wasn't seeing it at all.

She was, he thought, hardly for the first time, a beautiful woman. Her hair, today caught up at the back of her head with a clip in a tangle that was sexily untidy, had the multi-toned depth of a natural honey-blonde. And he didn't need to see her eyes to remember the deep, almost cobalt blue.

His fingers curled slightly, and he fought the urge to reach out and touch her. He'd felt the urge before, even a year ago, but knew it was wrong. Now, it was even stronger, that need. Just to brush his hand over her cheek, that's all, but he knew this wasn't the right time or place. Wondered if there ever would be a right time or place with this woman.

Wondered if he wanted there to be.

He hadn't meant to say it, but it somehow came

out anyway. "You're too good at what you do, you help too many people, to quit because of one case."

He thought he heard her suck in a quick breath. Then she looked at him, and he realized he had forgotten the depths of those eyes, and wished he could ease the remembered pain he saw there.

"Even if that case was your son?"

"You know what they told us. That Scotty was dead almost as soon as we started looking for him. Nobody could have found him in time to save him from that psychopath."

She looked at him for a long, silent moment. "You've come a long way," she finally said.

He made a short, sharp sound. "No. I'm as angry and bitter as I was when we found him. I've just focused the blame where it belongs."

She was quiet for a moment, then, in a flurry of movement she yanked open the passenger door and got out. She turned as if she were going to get into her own car without another word.

She made an odd, tight little sound and turned back. "I'm sorry we didn't find the killer."

"He eluded everyone. I talk to the detective who was on the case every month. There's never anything new."

"I should have kept going."

"You did. You kept going until Josh finally pulled you."

"I shouldn't have let him."

He hesitated a moment before saying "I told Josh to call it off."

She blinked. "What?"

"I told him to call it off. I know he would have gone on endlessly."

"But—"

He held up a hand. "I couldn't justify Josh pouring any more than he had into it."

She looked bewildered. "But Josh wouldn't have minded. He would have okayed the search to go on."

"It is going on. It's an open case with the police. And me."

She drew back slightly. "You?"

"I'll never stop."

"And if you find him? He's a murderer, Zach."

And I'm murderous, he thought. "I'm aware of that," he said, his voice much lighter than his thought.

As he watched her get into her car, her question echoed in his mind. He rarely thought about what he would actually do if—when—he found his son's killer. But when he did, there was little doubt of what he wanted to do to the man who had butchered his little boy.

"Zach?"

She'd rolled down the window and was looking at him. "I'm heading back to the foundation," he said.

"Fine. Zach, it won't do anybody any good if you end up in jail."

"Don't plan to," he said. Don't care, he thought. "Can we just work and not talk about this?"

Reeve winced. "All right," she said stiffly.

He watched her drive away, thinking that if he kept this up, the right place or time wouldn't ever be an issue.

"Look out," Sasha whispered to Reeve as she came through the front door of the foundation.

"What's up?"

Sasha nodded toward the small lobby area, where a dark-haired woman stood with her back to them. She was thin, wrapped in a jacket as if even a comfortable room temperature felt cold to her. Her hair was shoulder-length and wavy, and looked a bit tangled.

The woman must have heard them talking, because she turned to look. A puzzled frown creased her forehead as her gaze locked on Reeve, and Reeve smothered a startled gasp of recognition. In that moment the door opened again, and Zach walked in. The woman's attention shifted.

"I need to talk to you!" she said loudly.

Reeve saw Zach's face change as he registered his ex-wife's presence, going from a somewhat thoughtful expression to one that was studiedly neutral. She also sensed the change in his body, could almost feel the tension suddenly radiating from him. He flicked Reeve a sideways glance but kept moving, changing his direction to approach the lobby.

"Of course, Deborah." He said it politely, but only earned himself a glare. His expression never changed as they left the lobby. In fact, the way his hand went to her back to guide her seemed gentle, solicitous.

"She's a peach," Sasha said after they'd gone out of sight into the back of the building.

Reeve knew Sasha wasn't mean or insensitive, so she spoke very gently. "She's the mother of a murdered child."

Sasha sighed. "I know, I know, and I try to remember that when she gets on a tear. But—"

When the young woman stopped, Reeve turned to look at her. "What?"

"Zach's the father of a murdered child."

It was Reeve's turn to sigh. "Yes. Yes, he is."

"And when she does this, it just drives him harder. And he can't go much harder than he already does. Nobody can."

"I know," Reeve said softly.

And she knew perhaps better than anyone here. She'd seen him push himself beyond any human limits, and then go on. She'd seen him go from hopeful to afraid to despairing, had seen this big, strong man fall to the ground and sob at the grim, bloody sight of the murder scene.

As she walked back to add her small bits of information to the whiteboard, she was amazed that he'd come back as far as he had. That he was able to run, and run well, this foundation. She admired his obvious determination to save others from the tragedy that had destroyed his own life. Even as she shuddered at the thought of what it must cost him, reliving his own tragedy day after day as he tried to prevent another.

And it made her feel rather soft and weak that he'd been able to channel his grief into an enterprise like this while she, who had only been the investigator, had been cut off at the knees and unable to work for months.

Of course, she'd felt like more than just the investigator back then. There had been so much time, while driving to follow up one lead or another, spent talking. She'd come to know the man. To admire him. He was the kind of man some thought didn't exist much anymore. A man of principle and courage, not blindly stubborn but tough enough to do what he had to.

And human enough to cry when it was all for nothing.

She always wanted to do her best for Josh, and for Draven. But this had been more. She'd wanted to bring Zach's little boy back to him safe and sound more than she'd ever wanted anything in her life. And she hadn't been able to do it.

She thrust aside those old thoughts with an effort

that was almost physical. She made herself add the information she'd gotten about Rod's friends and hangouts to the whiteboard. She was writing the last of it when she finally admitted she could no longer block out the sounds from the next room, Zach's office.

Deborah's voice was getting steadily more strident. This was an old, solid building, so the words were mostly muffled, but she could still hear her.

"...keep him safe...your son...useless."

There was a pause in which she heard nothing; either Zach wasn't answering—something for which she could hardly blame him—or his voice had gone in the opposite direction of his ex-wife's.

"Don't you tell me...you don't..." A longer pause, then a shouted, "Go to hell, Zach!"

A door slammed so hard the windows rattled. When a couple of minutes later she heard the roar of a car engine and the squeal of tires as a car rocketed out of the parking lot, Reeve realized she'd been standing there holding her breath. She let it out slowly, with a wondering shake of her head.

Just as the sound of the car died away, the door opened and Zach stepped in. He looked startled for a moment, as if he hadn't expected to find her there. She didn't think her face betrayed anything, but perhaps he'd learned to read her. His expression gave way to one of ruefulness, and she knew he'd realized she must have heard at least part of Deborah's explosion.

"Sorry about the…noise," he said.

Reeve gave him a half shrug, but couldn't quite stop herself from asking, "Is it…always like that?"

He imitated her gesture. "Pretty much."

"Why do you even deal with it?"

"She didn't used to be that way. She was happy, outgoing, loving…." He shook his head. "And she's Scott's mother. We went through that together."

"It must be hard to talk to her, she's still so angry."

"So am I. She just deals with it differently. I do this," he said, gesturing at the whiteboard.

"Have you asked if she wanted to help?"

"Of course. She said she couldn't bear it, and that I was an ass for even asking her."

"So she hasn't found an outlet."

"No."

"Except you."

"She needs someone to blame to survive." He shrugged, both shoulders this time. "I'm already in hell, so it might as well be me."

Chapter 8

"No, no calls from Rod or any of his friends, or anyone else. I don't know anything more than I did this morning," Phyllis Durbin said, her tone peevish.

"Perhaps I should have mentioned we'll be checking with you frequently," Zach said smoothly. "It's part of our procedure. We know you want to be kept informed."

"You could do a little less informing and a little more finding," the woman snapped.

Somehow, whenever he'd just been through a blast from Deborah, other people's temper was easier to ignore. It reminded him they only had the power to sting if he allowed them to.

“We’re working on it round the clock,” he told her.

By the time Zach extricated himself and hung up, Bedford was back from his meeting with his old friends at the sheriff’s office. The man was invaluable for those contacts alone, but Zach had come to like and respect him for the dedicated man he was behind the gruff-seeming exterior.

“Ready,” he said to Zach. “And they had something.”

“Meeting!” Zach called out to the building at large.

The team began to gather in the war room to hear what the ex-cop had to say.

“Cops stopped the kid Friday, out on Pacific View Drive,” Bedford said.

Must have been one of those bits of little trouble his mother mentioned. “When?” Zach asked.

“Fourteen hundred hours,” he answered.

“So, before school was out,” Sasha mused.

“But two hours after he was last seen at school,” Zach said.

“And thirty minutes before he was supposed to meet Chuck and Patrick at the arcade,” Reeve said.

She sensed Zach go still, and knew he’d quickly picked up on the ramifications of that timing. Bedford wasn’t far behind.

“So he went missing between two and two-thirty?” the ex-cop said.

"So it would seem," Zach said softly.

"That narrows things down considerably," Sasha said. "unless it's a snatch in somebody's presence, we usually don't get such a small window."

"Was he driving his own car?" Reeve asked.

Bedford nodded.

"Was he cited?" Reeve asked.

Bedford nodded again. "His bad luck, that cop had given him a break twice before."

"Third time's the charm," Russ chirped. Sasha gave him a disgusted glance.

"Why?" Reeve asked. "Why did he get off twice?"

Bedford shrugged. "If I had to guess, I'd say he dropped Josh's name. It carries a lot of weight around here."

"Ironic," Reeve said, "since Josh Redstone is the last person on earth who would ever throw that weight around."

"Whatever the reason Rod got cited this time," Sasha said, "it's good for us."

"Did the police put together the timeline?" Reeve asked.

"They will now," Bedford said neutrally.

Reeve saw Zach give the man a quick grin, and knew that Bedford would make sure of that. He was clearly a valuable asset to the foundation. Zach had told her the man enabled them to work alongside the official authorities without stepping on any toes. It was largely due to Frank Bedford that the foundation enjoyed the high level of cooperation they had with local law enforcement on all levels.

"Can you talk to the officer who cited him?" Reeve asked.

Bedford nodded. "I've already got a call in to him. Turns out I worked with his brother a few years back."

"Good," Zach said. "He might have noticed something that didn't seem important at the time."

Bedford nodded.

"Anything else?" Zach asked.

"Rod is not only in trouble at school," Sasha said. "He's on the verge of a suspension."

"What kind of trouble?" Russ asked.

"Something about a confrontation with another student. That's all they'd tell me."

"Did it turn into a fight?"

"Sort of," Sasha said with a half shrug. "I talked to the vice-principal, and I got the impression Rod didn't throw any punches. That he left."

"Good for him," Zach said.

"When did this happen?" Reeve asked.

Sasha grimaced. "That's the thing. It happened Friday morning, before he disappeared."

"So," Russ mused aloud, "could be he just didn't want to go back to school and run into this kid again."

"Puts a whole new spin on it," Zach agreed.

"Got the other kid's name?" Reeve asked. "I can go see what I can get from him."

Sasha nodded. "Got your PDA? I'll beam it all to you." Reeve grabbed it from the outside pocket of her bag and turned it on.

While the information was beaming from Sasha's unit to hers, Bedford spoke again.

"I'm going to check in with the missing persons detective, Tigard, again," Bedford said. "Probably won't have anything, but I can give him what we've got on the new timeline."

Zach nodded. "Want to keep on their good side. Point is to find Rod, not who gets the credit."

Reeve had the feeling that was a refrain they'd heard before. It fit with what she knew of Zach, and with the philosophy of Redstone in general.

Speaking of which, she was due to give Josh a report. Not that he'd asked her to report to him, but she felt she should. She walked back to the small office Zach had told her to make her own while she was here. She pulled out her cell and hit the speed dial for Josh's office.

"St. John."

Josh's right-hand man's voice was brisk, as usual. And alert; even over the phone he gave the impression that he was hearing the things you weren't saying. She wondered if you called him in the middle of the night if he would sound the same. Given the rumors that he never slept anyway, she supposed he would.

"We've narrowed the disappearance timeline,"

she said, not wasting time with niceties that would only irritate St. John anyway. Her phone told him who was calling, and he knew what she was working on, so there was no point.

"To?"

"Between two and two-thirty Friday afternoon."

St. John didn't ask how they'd done it; he, as did all of Redstone, had complete faith in the abilities of the vaunted security team.

She wasn't sure she still deserved that faith, but she didn't demur; this wasn't the time.

"Anything else?"

"Nothing concrete. But threads are appearing."

She didn't ask him to relay the information to Josh; St. John would do what he thought best, and he would be right. Reeve had never heard the full story behind how the two men had connected in the early days, but Redstone legend had it that it had begun with a fistfight. Some thought it had been over Josh's wife, but Reeve was fairly sure it had happened before Josh had even met the woman he was to love so passionately and lose so painfully.

"I'll check back if anything new develops."

"Good." There was the briefest of hesitations, a pause that would have been barely noticeable in anyone else, but shouted because it was St. John. "Welcome back, Reeve."

He hung up before she could respond, which was just as well, since she couldn't think of a thing to say. She sat there with the phone in her hand for several stunned seconds after he'd disconnected. Her first coherent thought was to wonder if the man was ill. St. John never descended into the personal. Ever. He was steady as a rock, anyone from Redstone could count on him for anything, but it was also general knowledge that *rock* was the right word for a man who appeared to have all the emotion of granite.

Yet she couldn't doubt the sincerity of his words. It had been in his voice, in the faintest hint of softness beneath the cool, efficient tone.

It wasn't until she was on her way to Rod's school that the full import of what he'd said struck her.

Was she back?

She hadn't thought about it. She'd made a vow simply to focus on the job at hand, telling herself she could retreat when it was done, that this was simply a favor to Josh, not a request to go back to work.

But now, forced to think about it by St. John's unexpected comment, she had to admit she'd slid back into her old mindset, was working to the old rhythm, regaining the process. At first she'd thought she was just running on instinct, not really involved, just going through the motions. But somehow, going through the motions had become the real thing, the thing that had made her good at her job.

The thing that had made Draven consider her the go-to person for missing persons.

Maybe she was back. Or at least, ready to think about coming back. She wasn't sure what had done it. She suspected watching Zach, who had a hundred times the reason to be haunted as she herself had, drive himself with utter dedication to this cause had a lot to do with it. The admiration she'd always felt for him had morphed into something else, something even warmer, bigger. Something she didn't dare think about.

She arrived at the school, and was a little surprised at how easy it was to find Kyle Reid, the boy Rod had had the altercation with. She'd checked in with the principal, who directed her to the small auditorium across the quad area.

"He's in detention," the woman had said. "Again."

"That's a regular thing?" Reeve asked.

"Sadly, yes."

"Did he start the altercation with Rod Durbin?"

"I can't say that. No adult was present at the start."

"And the kids?"

A grimace flashed across the woman's face, brief but unmistakable. "When Kyle is involved, it's amazing how quiet everyone gets. Even some of the teachers."

She immediately looked as if she regretted her words, and shook her head sharply. "Mr. Linder has detention today. At least he keeps thing under control."

Apparently Kyle Reid's reputation spanned every strata of the high-school social structure, Reeve thought as she headed toward the building the principal had indicated.

Mr. Linder turned out to be a short, stocky man who had a no-nonsense air about him and a tough glint in his eye that made the principal's words seem quite believable. As did the fact that the kids, who began to stir as she walked in, stayed silent for the most part, except for one lone wolf whistle she chose to ignore. She explained who she was, and why she was there.

"You sure?" he asked when she told him who she needed to see.

"That bad, huh?" she asked with a wry quirk of her mouth.

"'Fraid so," he said with a similar expression. "But if you must."

"'Fraid so," she echoed, earning a smile.

"All right." He turned to face the room. There were a half dozen or so kids scattered around the room, apparently arranged so there was the greatest possible distance between them.

"Reid! Up front."

If she hadn't already picked out the boy in the back corner, the way the other kids' heads whipped around to stare at him would have told her this was Kyle Reid. He wasn't a particularly large boy for sixteen, but there was something about him that made Reeve think *bully.*

The minute he realized he was the center of attention, Kyle's wary look changed to a smirk as he rose and strutted toward the front of the room. Catcalls and whistles followed him, and only seemed to increase his display of bravado.

"Pick it up. Lady wants to talk to you," Linder told the boy who was taking his time strolling through the desks.

"Any time," Kyle said with a leer at her, his effort to sound like a man used to women wanting to talk to him failing completely. His fellow detainees seemed impressed, however, and a couple of more whistles echoed through the room.

"She's an investigator, Reid, so watch your mouth," Linder said when the boy finally arrived before them.

Something flickered in Kyle's eyes. "What kind of investigator?"

"Private," Reeve said. "Which is where I'd like to talk to you."

"Huh?"

"In private," she said.

"Oh."

"Use my office," Mr. Linder said, gesturing to a door behind him.

"Thanks," Reeve said.

Kyle hesitated, and Reeve didn't miss the mutinous look that began to spread across his face.

"If we talk in private," she said quietly, "then nobody out here has to know what we talked about. You can tell them whatever you want."

The look slowly faded as he thought this over, and after a moment the boy followed her into the office without complaint.

"What's this about?" he demanded after she shut the door behind them.

"Rod Durbin."

The boy snorted. "That loser."

"Don't like him?"

"What's to like? He's what got me stuck in here."

"I heard you two had a fight."

"Fight? That wimp? He's a jerk. Thinks a fancy car makes him cool."

"Takes more than that, doesn't it?" Reeve agreed.

"He'll never be cool."

"Once a jerk, always a jerk?"

"Yeah."

"He want to hang around with you?"

"Oh, yeah, like I'd let him. I told him to get lost and stay there. And he had to run off and tattle like some little baby. Said I hit him."

"Did you?"

"No."

"Try to?"

"No."

"Shove him, maybe?" The boy gave her a look that made her add, "Sounds like he might have had at least that coming."

"He did," Kyle said.

It wasn't an admission, but Reeve guessed she'd come close to the truth. "So what did you do when he came around again?"

"He didn't. I haven't seen him since."

Reeve didn't say anything. She watched as the boy processed thought. Finally his brows lowered as he looked at her.

"Hey, what's he saying I did now?"

"He's not saying anything, Kyle," she said softly.

The brows lowered further. "What's that supposed to mean?"

"He's missing. And you were one of the last people to see him."

It took him a moment; speedy thinking was clearly not his strong suit, but he got there.

"Wait a minute, I didn't do nothing to him! I never saw him after that, I told you."

"Well, if you had done something to him, you probably wouldn't tell me, would you?"

That one was almost beyond him, it seemed. His forehead creased. Then cleared.

"Wouldn't if I had something to hide. I don't."

Reeve studied him for a moment. "Nothing about Rod, anyway," she said.

The startled look he gave her then told her he did indeed have things to hide. It also told her how he reacted about those things. And her gut was saying he was telling the truth about Rod.

"Who else might have a beef with him?"

The inelegant snort again.

"Who doesn't? Told you, he's a jerk. Always mouthing off. Saying we'll be sorry, that someday we'll want to hang with him. As if."

"So, if you had to guess, where would he go?"

"Go?"

"If he wanted to hide. From you."

He seemed rather pleased by that idea. "Probably off with his geek friends."

"Checked that already," Reeve said with a shake of her head.

"Then I don't know. Don't care, either."

She believed him. He didn't look or sound like anything other than a bully who didn't like much of anything, or anyone, including himself.

Not a kidnapper.

Not a killer.

Chapter 9

Reeve didn't much like what she was thinking, but she couldn't seem to get the idea out of her head. It certainly wasn't the worst scenario, in fact, it was better than many grim possibilities. But she still didn't like the thought, because she knew what the ramifications were, knew what it would mean.

She pondered it as she drove back to the foundation offices. It had been a long day of following up leads that had come in on the tip line, leads that hadn't gone anywhere. It was late, had been dark for a couple of hours, and, she admitted, she was tired. Her endurance, always before a matter of pride—and demanded by John Draven—was definitely not what it once had been.

She was well into a mental plan of how to rectify that before she realized it hadn't been very long ago that she'd noted the deterioration of her once-peak physical condition without caring.

It hadn't been very long ago that she hadn't cared about anything.

She wasn't sure when the change had happened. Perhaps it had been when Josh asked for a favor. Or more likely it had been when she'd seen Zachary Westin throw himself into the hunt like a hungry tiger. Zach, who had more right to withdraw from the world than she ever had, but instead had plunged forward, devoting himself to the effort to save other parents from the nightmare he'd endured.

The parking lot at the foundation was empty except for one vehicle. Zach's, as usual; he was always the last to leave. Although the lobby was dark, the front door was unlocked and she was able to slip quietly inside. She saw the faint glow of light from the back and headed that way. She'd thought the light was coming from the war room, but instead found it spilling out from Zach's office. She paused in the doorway and glanced in.

He sat at his desk, his head propped up by one hand as he stared down at the stacks of papers spread across the surface. His eyes were hidden by his hand, but the slumped lines of his lean body told her he was as tired as she was. Maybe more so.

Maybe even asleep, she thought with a half smile.

She took a quiet step into the room, intending to wake him gently and send him home to rest. He didn't look up, and she wondered if perhaps he really had dozed off.

And then she saw what he was looking at.

Her smile vanished when she saw the pages of notes written in her own hand. The copies of official police reports. And there, buried beneath the pile, the edges of several photographs.

Photographs.

She didn't have to see them; she knew what they were. Didn't have to see them to know what they showed. Didn't have to see them because the grim, awful images were etched into her mind so deeply she knew she'd carry them to her grave.

How could he look at them? How could he even be in the same room with those horrible memories? She was across the room from them, safely distant, and she found herself looking at them as if they were a coiled rattlesnake.

She didn't think she'd made a sound, but he looked up. And in those green eyes, she saw all the hideousness he'd lived through. Saw the fear, the horror, the exhaustion. Saw the echo of the agony that had swamped him when they'd walked into his own garage and found disaster.

"Anything new?"

His voice was calm. Remarkably calm, she thought, considering what was spread across his desk. She knew it wasn't because that grim record didn't disturb him; he'd felt the brutal loss of his child too deeply ever to recall it with any equanimity.

It hit her then. He was calm the way a doctor confronting the latest in an endless stream of gunshot wounds is calm. When you've seen enough, you quit thinking about the details and focus on what had to be done.

He'd done this before.

"Reeve?"

"How often do you do this?"

To his credit, he didn't pretend to misunderstand. "Whenever it occurs to me I haven't for a while," he answered.

She wanted to ask how often that was, but she had a feeling it was more often than she wanted to know.

He studied her for a moment before saying, "Sasha thinks I'm crazy. A masochist."

Slowly, Reeve shook her head. "No. I understand."

Hadn't she done it often enough herself? She didn't have the file, but she didn't need it. She remembered it well enough. Too well. And sometimes the memories overwhelmed her defenses and she went through it all again, step by step. Just like he had been doing.

"I thought you might."

There was something in his voice, in the soft, gentle way he said the words, that made something tighten unbearably in her chest. She sank down into one of the chairs opposite his desk and stared at her hands.

"I never expected that." His voice was more normal now. "The police, they stayed...professional. Businesslike through the whole thing."

She had to swallow hard before she could talk. And she still couldn't look at him. "They have to. To you, it's your life, to them, it's one of a string of missing children they have to deal with."

"I know. If they let themselves get emotionally involved on every case, they'd go insane and not be able to help anyone."

She nodded.

"But you," he said, and his voice had gone soft again, "you were emotionally involved from the beginning."

"You were Redstone. Family."

He was silent for a long moment. She risked a quick glance at him, and the expression on his face brought back the tightness in her chest.

"It was more than that," he said at last. "You didn't run yourself into the ground, go without sleep for days, push the cops to work just as hard, and hold my hand every step of the way just because I was Redstone."

That tightness broke then, releasing all the emotions it had been blocking. And finally, she lifted her gaze to his face.

"No," she agreed. "I did it because I fell in love with Scotty the moment you showed me that picture of him, the one with the baseball cap on sideways."

There had been something so vivid and alive about the child in that photograph, something so innocent, as if he were a child of an earlier world when all there was to worry about was breaking a window with the baseball he held.

"And," she added, "I wanted to help his father. I wanted to help the father who had helped make that boy who he was, bright, confident...but still innocent. I know what kind of involvement that takes, how much time and care. And love."

"Reeve," he began, but stopped when she shook her head.

"I never wanted to help anyone more. And I never failed more."

"It wasn't your fault."

"He's just as dead as if it was. And I'll live with that every day, and with the nightmares of finding him...that way, every night."

Something changed in his face then. And his voice had a hollow, painful note when he spoke.

"I don't have nightmares."

She blinked, startled.

"I have long, beautiful dreams. Dreams of Scotty

alive, laughing, playing, sleeping with that cap on his head. Dreams of him nagging me to play catch when I least had time for it, dreams of him running to me when he was hurt or upset, because only I could make it right."

He stopped abruptly, as if the stream of words had hit an impenetrable barrier. And she knew then that he suffered his own kind of guilt still, the guilt of a father who hadn't been able to protect his own son.

"And then you wake up," she said softly.

His eyes closed, and the pain she saw in his face then put her own to shame.

"And then I wake up."

She reached out to him instinctively, wanting to ease his pain more than she wanted her next breath. She felt herself move, stretch her hand out toward him. Saw that hand tremble.

"Zach," she whispered.

His eyes snapped open. Focused on her hand, extended across the papers and pictures that held the destruction of his world. For a moment, nothing happened.

And then, just as she was about to retract her hand in embarrassment, he took it. Held it. His fingers curled around hers, and she felt the flow of…something, up through her wrist and arm, something warm and electric, as if a current had been established between them.

Her gaze flicked to his face, and the hint of puzzlement in his eyes told her he was feeling it too. For a moment longer neither of them moved. And when they did, she wasn't sure if it was she who had pulled her hand back, or he who had abruptly released her. And that quickly, the flow of whatever it was between them vanished.

He stared down at his desktop, but Reeve wasn't sure he was really seeing what was there. That he periodically put himself through the same kind of self-torture she did by reliving the tragic details made her feel…she wasn't sure what it made her feel. Empathy, certainly. A renewed pain of her own.

But above all she felt the need to help.

"May I take this, please?" she said, indicating the file spread across the desk.

His gaze snapped to her face. "What?"

"The file. May I look at it for a while?"

His expression asked "Why would you want to?" but given that she'd found him doing the same, he apparently didn't feel he had the right to voice the question.

"I…"

She sensed his resistance, gauged it, and thought she could push past it. "I'll get it back to you," she said, gathering up the papers before he could actually give her an answer. When she had them all tucked back into the worn manila envelope he obviously stored them in, she looked at him again. The exhaustion had broken through now, and he looked weary beyond belief.

She knew if she suggested he go home and get some sleep he'd shrug and say he was fine. It had happened often enough in the search for his son that she knew she needed a different approach.

"Walk me to my car, will you? It's late."

He blinked. "Oh. Okay."

As she'd hoped, his innate gentlemanliness kicked in and he automatically got to his feet, obviously without thinking about the fact that she was Draven-trained and well able to take care of herself, dark or not.

And also as she'd hoped, he locked up behind them. Since she now had the task he'd planned to spend the night on in her hands, perhaps he didn't see any point in staying.

Not that she wanted it, she thought as she felt the thickness of the envelope in her hands, the weight of the papers documenting the futile search. But if it got him to go home and get some sleep, she'd take the damned thing home and keep it there.

And end up doing the same thing he does, she thought. Drag it out as punishment.

"Thank you," she said as they reached her car. She unlocked it, dropped the file onto the passenger seat, and then turned back to face him.

"No problem."

"Get some rest," she suggested. "We'll start fresh in the morning."

He braced himself with one hand on the roof of her car as he faced her. He gave her a long look, and then understanding spread across his face.

"So that's what this was about."

It wasn't a question. Reeve didn't try to deny it. "You need rest."

"Mmm."

"I don't care if you agree, as long as you do it."

His mouth quirked upward. "Still a mind reader, Ms. Fox?"

"I never was."

"That obvious, am I?"

She had to think about that for a moment. Was he? Or was she simply able to read people? Or, more unsettling, was it simply him that she was able to read? That thought—

He kissed her.

One moment he was looking down at her with that odd, quirky smile, and the next his lips were on hers, warm and persuasive. The current that had flowed between them was re-established just that quickly, and the sound she made that she'd meant to be a protest, instead came out sounding like a moan of pleasure.

She'd always found him attractive. And perhaps she'd had to spend some time convincing herself back then that being attracted didn't necessarily have to follow. The fact that he was a man in crisis had made it easy to stay on the proper side of that line.

But now, in this moment, with his mouth doing insane things to every nerve she had, she had no idea where that line was.

Almost as suddenly that tempting warmth was gone. He straightened up, and she stared at him. He looked bemused as she struggled for what to say.

"No," was what came out.

His brows lowered. "Is that to the kiss, or me in general?"

"No, you're not obvious," she managed, with some effort, to say. "I never saw that coming."

The odd little smile came back. "You know," he said, the husky undertone in his voice sending a shiver up her spine, "neither did I."

It was the file, Zach told himself as he punched his pillow one more time. The pressure had built up, as it always did, until he had to drag it out and go over it all again, reliving the nightmare anew. He knew on some level that he was compelled to do it out of the guilt he still felt. And although it had taken him a while, he'd finally realized the compulsion came upon him whenever he'd gone too long without thinking about it, as if his conscience was reminding him he had no right to peace, not while his son's killer still walked free.

So he'd been off balance anyway, with every emotion brought to the surface as it always was when he went through that damned file. And then she'd been there, so close, looking up at him with that worried look. He knew others worried about him, his father, the staff here at the foundation, Josh. But somehow it was different coming from Reeve. Perhaps because they'd shared the nightmare so closely.

And apparently still did, he thought, remembering what she'd said about her own dreams.

Maybe it was that, too. But whatever it was, no one had been more surprised than he was when the irresistible urge to kiss her had come over him. That he'd gone ahead and done it had startled him even more.

Maybe she'd been right, he thought as the first drifting sensation of sleep began. He was just tired.

The memory that he'd wanted to kiss her before, and often, didn't manage to intrude before he slipped off completely.

This time when he dreamed of Scotty, Reeve was there with him, sharing the dread of awakening, and somehow the sharing lightened the burden.

When he woke up the room was light, and the usual waking pain was numbed by surprise. Usually he was up, showered and on his way out before the sun cleared the horizon.

When he glanced at the clock on the small,

bright-red nightstand that had come out of Scotty's room, he blinked in disbelief. But the combination of the sunlight and the numbers—7:03—were undeniable; for the first time in years he'd overslept. He felt better than he had in a long time; he'd almost forgotten what it was like to feel truly rested.

He was in front of the mirror shaving when he remembered the dream. He felt the sting as the razor blade nicked and realized his hand had jerked. For a moment he just stood there, staring at his reflection in the mirror. He didn't look any different, he thought. So why did he feel as if something momentous had happened inside him?

He shoved the sensation away, burying it beneath the rush of making up time. He finished quickly, dressed, and headed for the living room of his small apartment. Only then did he hear the voicemail tone ringing out from his cell phone. He usually brought the thing into the bedroom with him, but he'd forgotten last night.

He found it on the counter of his tiny kitchen. When he picked it up and looked at the screen, he felt a sudden clutch of fear. Three messages, five calls missed, all beginning at five this morning. Something had happened.

He flipped open the phone. Looked at the inner screen that displayed the last call.

Reeve.

For an instant he was back in that hell of a year

ago, when every time he got a call, he had hoped it was her and prayed it was not, at the same time.

Even as his mind recoiled from the stabbing memories, his thumb went to push the button to retrieve the messages, first one first.

"Zach, it's Reeve." Her voice, with the husky timbre that had always made him imagine waking up to it in the morning, held a note of urgency, and he again swore at himself for oversleeping.

"Rod hasn't been found, alive or otherwise, but there's been a development. Call me or the foundation office."

He spared a grateful thought for Reeve, for so quickly eliminating the worst possibility in her message. He pushed the return call button as he grabbed up his keys and ran to his car.

"Fox."

Indeed, he thought. "It's Zach. What's up?" This wasn't the time for explanations of his tardiness, so he didn't say anything.

Her voice was tight, clipped, when she answered him succinctly.

"Josh got a ransom demand."

Chapter 10

Five million or he dies. Tomorrow. Be ready for instructions.

Kidnapping.

The entire situation had escalated in one big jump, Reeve thought. And now she was relieved she'd kept her obviously erroneous thoughts to herself.

The group was gathered in the war room, waiting while Zach was brought up to speed.

"Big," Zach murmured as he reread the seven word e-mail that had been sent to Josh, "but not."

"Yes," Reeve agreed, understanding. Five

million was huge to most people, but to Josh Redstone, to Redstone, Incorporated, it wasn't an hour's operating costs.

Zach glanced up at Bedford. "The police know?"

The man nodded. "They were with Josh, set up on his phones in case it came in a call. He handed the e-mail over as soon as he got it."

"Then we'll leave the ransom aspects to them. Those are toes we don't want to step on," Zach said.

"The address it came to is Josh's private one. Private being relative," Reeve said wryly. "A lot of people have it, so that's not going to narrow things down for us much."

"What about where it was sent from?" Russ asked.

"They'll be subpoenaing the ISP records on that account," Bedford said, indicating the copy of the e-mail. "I'll reach out to Detective Tigard again so we can find out as soon as they do."

"I'm going to call Draven," Reeve said. "See if he can find me a computer geek on staff who can backtrack to where this was sent from."

Zach nodded. "Good idea." He turned to Sasha. "Try whoever runs the computer lab at the high school. They must keep records on usage."

The girl lifted a brow at him. "You think a kid did this?"

"I don't think one didn't," he said.

She nodded and left for her office. Russ hesitated, glancing from Zach to the direction Sasha had gone, then back. Zach nodded at him, and the young man darted after her.

When they were alone, Zach let out a sigh. "I was hoping Rod had just run away."

"It was a possibility," she said. "He's a teenager, and every problem is the end of the world."

"But this—" he held up the copy of the e-mail "—makes it a whole new ball game."

She hesitated, then said what she'd been wondering about. "Kind of late in the game for a ransom note. He's been missing two days."

Zach looked at her. "Yes, a little. But not suspiciously. It's all in the mind of the kidnapper. If he thinks the mark will sweat more, he waits."

She nodded. "May indicate he's a game player."

"Might. It could also—"

The tap-tap of hard heels on the floor interrupted his words. They both looked toward the hallway the sound was emanating from. Reeve recognized Deborah Westin, and although they weren't standing close together, she instinctively took a half step back from Zach.

"Hello, Deborah," Zach said quietly.

The woman didn't speak, just turned suspicious eyes on them both. Reeve searched for a tactful way to retreat, but the woman was blocking the doorway.

"You again?" she said, frowning at Reeve.

"She's helping on a case," Zach said.

Deborah's gaze turned angry as it fastened on Zach. "You couldn't even be bothered to come this morning?"

Reeve saw a muscle in his jaw jump. "I told you I wouldn't."

"How could you? Didn't you love Scotty at all?"

Reeve's breath stopped in her throat. She should not be here for this, she thought, and took a step toward the door despite Deborah's presence. But a quick, barely perceptible shake of Zach's head stopped her.

"I loved him so much I'd rather remember the day of his birth."

It struck Reeve then. She hadn't realized that today was the one year anniversary of the day Scott Westin had vanished.

"You'd rather pretend it never happened!"

"If only I could," Zach said wearily. "I'm sorry, Deborah, I just don't feel gathering at his grave at every invented anniversary is the way Scotty would want us to remember him."

"I suppose you have a better idea?"

A sad smile lifted one corner of his mouth. "Sure. Go to a baseball game for him. Fly a kite. Remember how he loved that?"

All the anger seemed to drain out of her. She sagged, and for a moment Reeve thought she would go down. In a response too quick to be anything but instinctive, Zach jumped forward to prop her up.

"Oh, Zach." She let her head drop against his chest.

"I know, Deborah. Believe me, I know."

There was room now, in the doorway, and Reeve began to edge that way. This was not a scene she wanted to witness, for a variety of reasons. For now, Deborah was once more the woman Reeve remembered, unbearably sad and broken. Reeve felt guilty for not having more sympathy for the woman.

"I'm sorry, Zach," Deborah was saying, her voice muffled against him. "I don't mean to be this way, but…."

"I know you don't. It's not you."

"It's all that's left of me."

"Get some help, Deborah. Please."

She pulled back then. "Help?"

"Talk to someone. I can refer you to a counselor, or—"

"I'm not one of your…clients!" Deborah shouted, pushing him away.

As quickly as that, the anger was back. Radical mood swings were an effect of grief, Reeve knew, and continued her gradual approach to the door.

"And this is not some stranger's child we're talking about. How can you be so damned detached?"

Detached. Reeve stared at the woman, wondering how, even in grief, she could be so wrong.

Deborah seemed to really notice her for the first time, and Reeve wished she'd made it out the door first.

"What are you staring at?"

"He's not detached," Reeve said before she could stop herself. "He cares more than anyone I've ever known. If he didn't he wouldn't let you talk to him like this."

"Reeve," Zach said, his tone warning.

She let out a sigh. "I know. I'm sorry. And I'm leaving."

Deborah took a step back, and for a moment Reeve thought she meant to block her exit. But then she realized the woman's gaze was flicking from her to Zach and then back again.

"I should have seen this," she said, her voice beginning to rise again. "You two. Spending all that time together. What were you doing when you should have been looking for my son?"

"What?" Zach's tone was sharp and incredulous.

"It's true, isn't it?" Deborah said, still focused on Reeve. "You had an affair, didn't you? Instead of searching, you were seducing my husband! You're why my little boy is dead!"

Reeve recoiled, the accusation making her faintly queasy.

"That's enough, Deborah!" Zach took her by the shoulders and turned her away from Reeve. His voice was taut. "I loved our son more than my life.

And I loved you. Those are facts. Nothing you say now will change them. Go home. And get yourself another punching bag, I've had enough."

"Protecting her, like you didn't protect our son?"

"What happened to Scott wasn't my fault, and it certainly wasn't Reeve's. Get some help, Deborah. Before it's too late."

The woman he'd once loved jerked away from him, and gave him a furious glare. "I don't care what you do. I don't care what you did. If you two had an affair, and still are, I don't care. I beat you to it anyway."

"What?" Zach's brows furrowed.

"I had an affair with someone who loved me more than you ever did."

Ouch, Reeve thought.

"Ned especially loved Scotty, too, and he wanted us all to be together, as soon as I could divorce you. You didn't know that, did you?" she finished triumphantly.

"No," Zach said, and Reeve wasn't sure if he sounded hurt or bemused that he apparently hadn't had a clue.

"Serves you right," Deborah said, and then turned her back on him and walked away with her head low.

For a long moment Zach just stood there, staring after her. Reeve had no doubt that he hadn't known a thing about Deborah's affair. But then, neither had she; nothing had surfaced in her search for Scott.

"Has she remarried?"

Zach blinked and seemed to come back to the present. "What?"

"I just wondered if she'd remarried. Perhaps to…this Ned person."

"No. She hasn't."

When did they split? Reeve wondered. And where is he now?

And more important, she thought, why didn't Deborah say anything about another man in the picture when they'd been searching for Scott? Had they already been split long enough that she didn't think of it? Had she—

The ring of her cell cut off her thoughts. It was an unfamiliar Redstone number.

"Fox."

"Hi. This is Ryan Barton. Your computer geek."

He sounded so good-natured about it she knew he didn't take offense at the term.

"The soul of the new infrastructure," she said, and he laughed. "What have you got for me, Ryan?"

"That e-mail, through a pretty circuitous route through several servers, originated from the Javawire."

"The what?"

"It's a fairly new coffee-shop hot-spot, down by the beach on Waterfront Drive just off Coast Highway."

"Been there?"

"Yeah, couple of times, but it's usually too crowded for me."

"What's the setup?"

"Bring your own, or they have a half-dozen setups you can use. A free fifteen minutes comes with one of their expensive drinks."

"Do you have to register, give a name?"

"Nah. Anonymity, that's the name of the game in these places. Ups their business. They'd be able to tell you which computer was used, but not who used it. Unless they paid with a credit card, then they might be able to narrow it down to who used the machines within the time period of the e-mail."

"Thanks, Ryan."

"Sure. Want me to keep hunting?"

"For?"

"Maybe the route might tell us something. What servers he used. Might be something he does all the time. Maybe I can find out if he—or somebody—has used that same route before."

"Good thought. Thanks again."

"It's for Josh," the young man said simply.

"Yes," she said softly, "yes it is."

"You're smiling. Good news?" Zach asked when she closed the phone and put it away.

"A potential lead, but that's not why I'm smiling. I just like being Redstone. I'd almost forgotten."

Zach nodded. "I know. It wasn't easy for me to

leave, even knowing I—and the foundation—would still be part of the family."

"We'd all go a lot further than putting in some extra effort for Josh."

Zach was silent for a moment, looking at her, before he said quietly, "Some would even take a bullet for him."

She stiffened; she hadn't known he knew about that.

"You're part of the Redstone legend," Zach said.

"I was on bodyguard detail for that summit. So that's what I did."

"I thought it was only the Secret Service that was trained to get in front of bullets."

"You haven't worked for John Draven," she answered dryly.

He chuckled. "My loss, I suspect. But I'm very glad Josh is still with us."

"So am I. It would have been just too ironic if the man responsible for so much good had been taken out by that moonbat who never had a positive thought in his mind, who thought of nothing but tearing down and destroying."

"The bigger you get, the bigger the target on your back gets," Zach said.

"It's on your back because they don't have the guts to face you," she said wryly.

She was glad they'd gotten off into more esoteric territory than the bullet wound she'd suffered when she'd pushed Josh out of the line of fire. She hadn't really been expecting anything, the economic summit Josh had been at had gone remarkably smoothly. Josh didn't usually do much of that, but he'd been asked to speak by the President himself, who also happened to be a friend. And Josh rarely passed on a chance to help a friend.

She'd seen the group of protesters, in this case the kind who seemed to turn up at anything and everything, a fairly small group shouting against so many things she couldn't make out any single one, or track all the signs. But her job—Josh had been virtually ordered to bring security by his friend from the White House—had been to keep him safe.

Josh and Draven had long ago worked out and well publicized his policy that should anyone ever try to kidnap him, no ransom would be paid, and thus far it had worked. But that didn't mean he was safe, so when she'd seen the group she'd steered him out a side door of the hotel where the meetings were being held. They'd been almost to the rented car—they'd offered a limo, but Josh wasn't the limo sort—when it had happened. She'd heard something, and from the corner of her eye spotted a man in a heavy coat rushing toward them.

Instinctively she had shoved Josh into the vehicle, grabbing her weapon at the same instant. She turned back and caught a .38 slug just below her left rib cage. She returned fire, ending the threat with a single shot that felled the crazed shooter in his tracks.

She remembered the odd numbness, remembered Josh scrambling back out of the vehicle, saying her name and yelling orders to the staff and security. Remembered sliding down to the ground as hot, wet blood streamed through her fingers. And in her mind hearing Draven say at her funeral, "She got the job done."

Josh told her later she'd been smiling when she passed out.

"What was the lead?"

Zach's question snapped her back to the present. Quickly she told him what Ryan had said.

"I'm going to head down there, see if anybody remembers who was there at the time the ransom demand was sent."

"I'll drive."

Reeve hesitated, but saw no harm in it, so nodded. Besides, she wanted to probe some areas he might not want to discuss, and he couldn't walk away if he was driving.

It was only about a twenty-minute trip, so she knew she had no time to waste. As soon as they were out of the driveway she jumped in with both feet.

"Do you have any idea who Ned is?"

If the blunt, very personal question startled him, it didn't show beyond a sudden stillness.

"No," he finally said.

At least he hadn't told her it was none of her business, Reeve thought. As he well could have.

"Not even a guess?"

She saw his jaw tighten then. "I don't even know why, so how would I know who?"

Reeve wished she didn't have to do this, but her gut was telling her to keep going. "I can't imagine why, either," she said.

She hadn't meant it to sound quite so fervent. And he heard it, she knew by the way he glanced at her, his brows lowered as if he were trying to interpret her tone. She went on hastily.

"Nobody even remotely comes to mind? An acquaintance, somebody you both might know, or somebody she used to talk about with you and suddenly stopped?"

"Now that's a pleasant thought," he muttered.

"I know it's not," she said. "I can guess how it makes you feel about the woman you loved enough to marry."

He gave her that quick look again, as if he were trying to see if there was something more behind her words.

"I don't love her anymore, if that's what you mean," he finally said as they stopped at a red light.

Since her mind had been in another track altogether, she was startled.

At her silence, he looked over at her again. "Is that what you wanted to know?" he asked.

She realized then that, not being privy to the thoughts she'd had, he'd misunderstood her interest. He thought she'd been trying to find out if he still loved Deborah. And the moment she realized that, she sensed the difference in his demeanor. He was looking at her with the same amount of intensity, but there was something different about it, something more personal.

Interest? Speculation? Something more, deeper?

To her shock, a little thrill shot through her. That part of her had been numb for so long that it took her a moment to realize that what she was feeling was a spark—well, beyond a spark—of interest returned.

Scrambling, she managed to stammer, "I just… I wondered…if you had any idea who it might have been."

He had to see that he'd rattled her, but he was gracious enough to let it pass. He appeared to think about her question for a moment, but then shook his head.

"What does it matter now anyway?"

"I don't know that it does," she said, recovered now. "But it's something unknown cropping up long after the fact, and that bothers me."

That wasn't all, but she left it at that. Zach didn't need the distraction of her admittedly vague thoughts right now. Neither did she, for that matter. Right now, what mattered most was finding Rod safe and sound. And in that case time was of the essence.

And that time was ticking away.

Chapter 11

Zach wondered if he would have dared to throw out that feeler if Deborah hadn't accused him of an affair with Reeve. But she had, and the images that had paraded through his mind had been vivid and breath-stealing.

Not at all what Deborah had intended, he was sure.

Back during the search for Scotty, he'd been aware she was a very attractive woman, but every ounce of his being had been focused on finding his son. Besides, he'd been married, and he took that vow very seriously. There was never any question, then.

Now, he was even more aware. He knew he was

attracted to Reeve; it was hard to deny when his body kept reminding him. And when he'd kissed her…. He sucked in a breath at the heat that rocketed through him at the memory.

He didn't think he'd misunderstood that slight tightness in her voice when he'd asked her if she wanted to know if he still loved Deborah. It had been more than surprise or shock at the blunt question. He'd gotten to her, and there was only one way he could—or wanted to—interpret that. She—

"There it is," she said, derailing his thoughts.

He looked where she was pointing and saw a vividly red building amid the row of more staid edifices. A neon coffee-mug-shaped sign flashed in front, and there were several people clustered in the doorway and sitting at three outside tables.

He had to go a half block down to find a spot to park, even this early on a weekday morning.

"Happening place," he said.

"So it seems."

They had to thread their way in through what could only be called a crowd. The clientele seemed to run the gamut from middle-aged latte lovers who bought and left, to average-looking folks with laptops on tables, to young, pierced, wired types who congregated around the computer stations on the back wall.

They started with the harried baristas, two young women who stated emphatically they were too busy to talk or to notice who came and went. Always. They barely had time to acknowledge their own friends who came in. In fact, they were already behind by stopping this long to talk to them. The manager, Charlie, was in back if they wanted to check with him.

They found the office the one dark-haired girl had pointed toward, but were a bit startled at what—or rather who—they found. A young man with brown hair bleached blond at the tips and three earrings in his left ear, dressed in knee-length cargo shorts and a beach-scene T-shirt stood up.

"Need something?" he asked.

"Busy place," Reeve said, "nice job."

"Hope it lasts," he said with a grin. "It's a good gig."

When they told him what they wanted, he frowned. "I don't know if I can do that."

"We understand that you can only tell us if the person used a credit card."

"Well, yeah, but isn't this like an invasion of privacy? Don't you need a subpoena or something?"

Everybody's a lawyer, Reeve thought.

"We're not cops, Charlie," Zach said. "We don't care where anybody surfs here. We're just trying to find a kidnap victim."

"Kidnapped?" Charlie's eyes widened. "Serious?"

"As a hard-drive crash," Reeve said wryly.

"Ransom and everything?"

"And everything," she said. "Including a note. Sent from here."

His expression turned to one of shock. "Whoa!"

He started to go on but stopped, and Reeve wondered if in his excitement he'd been about to say something he realized was inappropriate. Something along the lines of "Cool!" she guessed.

"Let me get the credit card info," he said, sitting back in his desk chair and turning to his computer station. A few minutes later they had a printout including facsimile signatures of everyone who had used a credit card to pay for computer time from an hour before the ransom demand had been sent.

"Thanks, Charlie," Reeve said with a smile. The young man blushed, which she found rather charming.

"Any time. Can I get you a latte or something?"

"Not today," she said, "but thanks."

"Sure." He grinned suddenly. "It's nice to see a hot, non-geek girl in here now and then."

Reeve laughed.

Zach had been quiet throughout the exchange, although Reeve noticed an odd expression that had come over his face. A little beyond thoughtful. She wondered what he was thinking.

Then, as something else occurred to her, she took out the photograph of Rod and held it out to Charlie.

"Ever see him in here?"

There was no hesitation in his answer. "Sure. He's in a lot. Okay if he's alone, but with his buddies, he's a pain. Brags a lot, you know?"

She was beginning to. "When was the last time you saw him?"

"Last time I was here. Before the weekend. I've been off for three days."

His phone rang then, and Reeve quickly thanked him before they left the office. The two girls behind the counter glanced at the photo, agreed that he was a regular, but reiterated they didn't have time to track who came in when.

"I'd like about ten per cent of that place," Reeve said as they got back in his car.

"Seemed like he'd be willing to give it to you."

She drew back slightly at the change in his tone. "What?"

He gave her a sideways look as he slid the key into the ignition. "You made quite an impression."

What *was* that note in his voice? Surely he didn't care who got the information as long as they got it?

"Rapport," she said neutrally.

"There was certainly that." That sideways look again. "I can't testify as to your geekhood, but I can definitely agree to the hotness factor."

After a startled moment she felt her cheeks heat. Blushing didn't feel charming from this side, she thought, just flustering.

"Thanks," she said, feeling awkward.

She hadn't seen that coming. She supposed she should have, after The Kiss....

Funny, that was how she thought of it. The Kiss. As if there had been none before. But it had felt that way.

Because of the increased urgency brought on by the ransom demand, the subject of that fervent kiss hadn't even surfaced between them. It had been there, in the back of her mind, there was no way it couldn't be. But right now, they had to focus on getting Rod home safely.

Besides, she didn't like to overanalyze things like that. And didn't want to hit him with any kind of "What did that mean?" demands. It didn't have to mean anything. It simply was.

Boy, was it, she muttered inwardly.

When she was back in her borrowed office at the foundation, she called in to Josh's office.

"St. John."

"News?" Sometimes she played at trying to be as terse as he was; she rarely succeeded.

"No contact since the e-mail."

"Money?"

"Holding it."

Something belatedly occurred to her. She'd been so focused on this end of things that she hadn't thought about how this would look from the outside.

But she'd be willing to bet Draven had.

"If they insist Josh deliver the money himself," she began.

"Covered. Draven's on it. If it's a ruse to flush him out, it won't work."

"Good."

She gave St. John what little they had so far. After she'd hung up, she leaned back in the borrowed chair and settled down to think. Draven often said the most important work was sometimes just sitting and thinking, and she'd learned the lesson well.

She ran through everything in her mind, all the facts they'd gathered, impressions from the people she'd talked to. She mentally stacked them up against the various possibilities, to see where they meshed and where they diverged. And that gut feeling she'd quashed before rose up again, stronger now, and meshing in more places than any other theory.

"Damn," she muttered, but she couldn't stop thinking about it. Her mind was beginning to fixate, and she knew she needed to break the loop. She sat up and put aside Rod's file and picked up the thick, weighty stack with Scott Westin's name on it.

She hadn't looked at it before. She'd mainly asked for it to keep Zach from draping himself over it any longer. A wave of pain swept her as she opened it and saw the front photograph, the one that was as vivid in her mind now as it had been when she'd first seen it. That grinning, adorable six-year-old with the missing front tooth and the cockeyed baseball cap looked up at her, frozen in time.

The first time she'd seen it she'd looked forward to meeting the little boy. The last time she'd seen it the image had been blurred by her tears because she never would.

It hurts you this much, and you never knew him, she told herself. *Imagine how Zach feels.*

Steeling herself, she began to read through the file. She skipped the initial reports, she knew those by heart, and began with the various interviews. Reading Zach's had an extra poignancy now, knowing how he'd channeled his unrelenting grief. Reading Deborah's made it harder to believe the woman she'd just seen was the heartbroken woman so obvious in the statement. Whatever she'd become, whatever her grief had made her, she deserved more kindness and understanding than Reeve had given her, and she vowed to do better should she encounter Deborah again.

She went on to the rest of the interviews, coworkers of both parents, people from the child's school. Housekeepers, gardeners and the contractor and crew who had been doing a kitchen remodel on the vacant house next door. Neighbors, of special interest the ex-con on the other side, a man who'd served time for burglary and was now out and living with his grandmother.

They and the cops had spent a lot of time with Murray, pounding him with questions, checking out his story. He'd made the usual complaints about being harassed because he was an ex-con. He'd done his time, he should be left alone, and not always on the list of usual suspects.

"You're the one who wrote your name on that list," Reeve had told him flatly, feeling no sympathy.

His alibi had turned out to be another ex-con whose story had been shaky, but he never wavered from it, and they couldn't break it. They'd had to move on to other suspects.

She continued through the file, reclipping the statement of the landlord of the house next door with copies of the expired lease agreement for the house that was now being remodeled. The former tenant, attorney Gary E. Schumer, had moved out of state a couple of months before Scott had vanished, and the house had been empty at the time.

Then came a copy of a business card for Hammer Construction, a company name that had her wondering just how much effect Brent Hammer's name had had on his career choices. She remembered him; the young man who had recently taken over the business begun by his grandfather and expanded by his father had been appalled at the idea that she thought he might be involved. But pedophiles, as she well knew, were by necessity good actors.

With every page she turned she knew she was

coming closer to the photos. She'd already decided she wasn't going to look at them. Not so much because they added nothing she didn't already know, but because she didn't need to; she had her own set of vivid, obscenely perfect images, images that were seared into her mind forever.

She stopped at the last page of the last report, a Redstone form, saw her own shaky signature at the bottom of the admission of failure.

You couldn't have done more if he'd been yours. It's not your fault we didn't get there in time.

Zach's words, his absolution, echoed in her head. She'd spent so long blaming herself, she didn't know if she could let go of the guilt. It felt as if it had become part of her foundation, part of who she was. Crack Redstone Security agent, who screwed up the one case she wanted to do right.

It wasn't the only case that hadn't turned out exactly as she'd wanted, there were a couple of others. But every other one at least had had an acceptable outcome. An outcome the people involved, including her, could live with.

Not this one.

Tearing her mind out of that old, well-worn groove, she looked again at the thick file. She'd harbored some foolish hope that going through it again would trigger something, that some piece she'd missed, some clue she'd overlooked would pop out now, so much later.

It hadn't.

With a sigh she closed the file on Scott Westin and went back to her notes on Rodney Durbin, where she had no more clues, but a gut feeling she was trying to ignore.

"Meeting!"

Sasha's voice rang out in the hallway. Reeve glanced at her watch, surprised by how late it was, by how long she'd obviously been sitting here, pondering futilely.

She got up, put Scotty's file in a drawer and locked it since there was open access to the offices, picked up the other file and headed for the war room.

"Updates," Zach said briefly, nodding at Bedford.

"The police are still set up on Josh's phones at the office and at home. There's been no call with instructions. No contact at all since the initial e-mail."

All of which Reeve already knew from St. John, but she said nothing.

"The school records show Rod used a computer in the lab there the morning before he disappeared," Sasha said. "From what I could find, he'd visited a couple of automotive Web sites, looking for car accessories, and sent two e-mails, one an answer to an incoming one from another car parts house, and one to a kid named Patrick."

"One of his arcade buddies," Reeve said.

"Reeve and I learned he's also a regular at the computer café the ransom e-mail was sent from."

"You think maybe the kidnapper grabbed him there?" Sasha asked the room in general. "If he was a regular, and the guy knew his habits…."

"Could be," Zach said.

"I don't get it," Bedford said. "The kid's got a state-of-the-art computer set-up at home, why's he using all these other computers?"

"I think it's partly a social thing," Reeve explained. "That café is quite the hot spot for more things than e-mail."

"Oh."

"Besides," Sasha said, "they have the one thing home doesn't have."

"What's that?" Zach asked.

"Freedom from parents," the girl said with a grin.

"There is that," Reeve agreed, laughing.

Zach said nothing, but Reeve's laugh died away as she realized this was a man who would never be dealing with his son's teenage problems. And that he would probably give up everything for just one rip-roaring fight with a teenaged Scott over… anything.

She didn't want to look at him, didn't want to see the pain in his eyes again. She stared at the white-board, rapidly filling with various colored bits of information beneath the large header Rodney J. Durbin.

Rodney J., she thought. Named for Josh. Out of respect? Or something more…mercenary?

By all accounts, Elizabeth Redstone had been a gentle, loving, honest and down-to-earth woman, all these positive qualities leavened with a healthy helping of wit and astuteness. She'd been so remarkable that Josh had withstood countless efforts on the part of many to change his solitary status. He'd loved Elizabeth until the day she died and beyond, and that alone spoke volumes about the kind of woman she had been.

Could her sister be so very different?

She'd hate to pry into an area so painful for Josh, but she might have to if something didn't break soon.

Five million or he dies…

That would be even more painful for Josh, she thought, and steeled herself to make a call to him to ask some questions about his sister-in-law.

"Rodney J. Durbin," she murmured to herself, reading the top of the board again.

A memory hit her with an almost palpable force. And the instant the meeting was over, she headed quickly back to her temporary office, unlocked the desk drawer, and pulled out Scotty's file once more.

She dug through it until she found what she wanted. Then she sat down at the computer and did some quick searching. It didn't take her long to find out what she'd wanted to know. Or didn't want to know.

But there it was. And now that she had it, she didn't know what to do with it. Didn't know what to do because she knew what it would mean, what it would do, in particular to Zach, if she was right. If this was more than just coincidence.

The strength of her recoil from that idea, from the thought of being the one to hurt him all over again, startled her.

God, she couldn't tell him. She just couldn't. She couldn't bear to see that old wound, not yet healed anyway, ripped open again. And she couldn't bear being the one to do it.

But neither could she let this go. And in case she was wrong, she'd better tread carefully. And who better to tread carefully than the ultra-secretive, ever-careful St. John? She made the call, told him what she wanted, and why she wanted him to do it. He merely listened, asked one question, and then told her to wait for his call.

Bless you, St. John, she thought.

Josh's right-hand man might be reclusive and laconic to a fault, but he was scary-smart and had connections who had connections in a seemingly endless line. If information was out there to be found, he'd find it.

If.

Just wait, she told herself. You can't do anything more about it now. And you don't have anything yet. It could be coincidence. Chances are it is.

She managed to convince her mind.

Her gut wasn't buying it.

She looked up just as the object of her concern stuck his head in the door.

"We just got lucky," Zach said.

"What?"

"Rod's ATM card was used in Huntington Beach less than an hour ago."

Chapter 12

"Nice rapport you folks have with the cops," Reeve said as Zach drove.

They should be at the bank the card had been used at in less than ten minutes, with clearance to watch the ATM video. Of course, Zach thought, it didn't hurt that Josh owned a sizeable chunk of said bank.

"They know we won't get in their way," he told her, "or do anything to compromise any case they might need to build. They also know we have the same central goal."

"Except they add capturing the suspect," she said.

"We don't exclude that, either." Zach glanced at her, then turned his eyes back to the road. "The fact that we're Redstone doesn't hurt. You guys in security have quite the solid reputation with every law-enforcement agency around."

"Thank Draven for that," Reeve said. "He's worked long and hard to make that the case around the world. Wherever Redstone has an operation, Draven's been there paving the way for us long before we ever actually have any case to work on."

Draven was one of a kind, Zach knew. But then, according to Redstone lore, all of the security team were. Most Redstone people wouldn't recognize them if they saw them, on purpose on Draven's part, he knew. But they knew about them. Knew that as much as it was their job to keep the bad apples out, it was also their job to protect and help everyone and anyone in the Redstone family. All who worked at Redstone knew that if they needed help, even if it wasn't directly related to their work, they could turn to Redstone Security.

Just as he had.

When Scotty had gone missing, when they could no longer deny that this was more than him just wandering off, his first call had been to the police.

His second had been to Redstone Security.

"Zach? Are you all right?"

He snapped back to the present, realized that, as usual, the memories had made him tense up, and his knuckles were white as his fingers clenched the steering wheel.

He relaxed them. "Fine."

She didn't believe him, he could see that with a quick look at her face. But she seemed content to have snapped him out of it, because she merely pointed up ahead.

"There's the bank."

He nodded, and moments later they were parking in the lot near the bank of ATMs on the side wall. There was what appeared to be an unmarked police car parked in the fire lane.

When they got inside they were directed to the bank manager's office. The video monitor was already set up, and a young woman in the uniform of the bank's security company was setting up the clip. Zach greeted Detective Tigard, and introduced Reeve.

"Heard a lot about you Redstone guys," the detective said as he took Reeve's offered hand.

Zach could almost hear him mentally adding, "But nobody told me they looked like you!" and he grimaced inwardly.

"The good stuff's all true," Reeve said with a smile at the man.

"All I've heard is good stuff," he assured her.

"We're ready," the security woman said, and Zach was childishly glad of the interruption. "The transaction started at eleven-fifteen," the woman said, "so I backed it up to two minutes before that."

All eyes were fastened on the small image. It showed the parking lot and one customer, an older man who walked out to a racy-looking little coupe and drove off. Then nothing for several seconds. Finally a young woman walked up, from the direction of the sidewalk, not the parking lot. The sunlight glinted off the three earrings in her left ear, and the one through the outer edge of her eyebrow.

"Well, well," Reeve said.

Detective Tigard reacted immediately, ordering the woman to stop the playback. "You know her?"

"Just met her today," Reeve said, studying the image of the brunette who had sent them back to Charlie's office. "She works at a hot-spot coffee shop down at the beach."

Zach, mindful of the necessity of maintaining good will with the police, quickly explained what they'd found out to the detective.

"No wonder she didn't want to talk to you," the detective said. "She's in on it."

"And Charlie said Rod was always bragging," Zach added. "Maybe he bragged about his rich uncle in front of the wrong person."

Reeve, Zach noticed, said nothing. In fact, she looked troubled. Maybe she didn't want to think of surfer boy being involved, he thought sourly. Sure, the kid was maybe ten years younger than she was, but like that kid had said, wasn't that the latest trend, younger men and older women?

Especially women who looked like Reeve, he muttered to himself.

Detective Tigard gestured at the monitor. “Let’s go on.”

The girl in the video studied the machine for a moment, as if she’d not used it before. Then she glanced around, although there was no one else in sight. She put the card, which she’d apparently been hiding in her hand, into the slot. She looked around behind her again before glancing down at a small piece of paper in her other hand when the PIN was requested. She punched the keys as requested for the maximum cash withdrawal.

The ATM accepted the number she keyed in and began to process, and a few moments later she had the wad of cash in her hand and shoved it into a small, leather purse. She glanced around once more, then left hastily back the way she had come.

“That’s it,” the security woman said. “No sign of her again.”

“How about before?” Reeve asked.

“I started looking a half an hour before this,” she said. “That was the first she’s appeared in that time.”

“Thinking she was there earlier, casing?” the detective asked Reeve.

“Maybe. Or, she was nervous enough, maybe it took her a couple of tries.”

“Good idea. Let’s go further back,” Tigard agreed.

“How far do you want me to go?” the security

woman asked, not sounding happy about the idea of watching endless hours of ATM video.

Detective Tigard hesitated, not looking too happy at the idea himself.

"We can do that," Zach offered, "if you can make us a copy of, say, the last twenty-four hours?"

The woman looked at the police detective. He nodded. "Thanks," he said.

"We've got the staff," Zach said with a shrug. "And you've got more important things to do."

"You'll let me know if anything turns up on it."

It wasn't a question, but Zach answered anyway. "Frank Bedford will be on the phone to you within seconds."

"Good enough," said with a nod. Then he added, "Bedford was a heck of a cop."

"I know," Zach said.

"We miss him. But he's happier now than I ever saw him before."

Zach smiled. "I'm glad to know that. He's a good man, and we'd be lost without him."

He meant it, too. Bedford filled his unique function of allowing a private agency to work hand in hand with the official one with efficiency and a surfeit of carefully maintained camaraderie with his former colleagues. And he did it without stepping on anyone's toes, and without making the police dread seeing him coming. Zach wouldn't want to have to find someone else to fill his shoes.

As they headed back to the foundation with the copy of the video feed for the twenty-four hours before the withdrawal, Zach thought he'd have to set up shifts of people to watch the whole stretch. But then he heard Reeve on the phone, to the same Redstone computer expert who had tracked the ransom e-mail.

"Question, Ryan," she was saying. "If we have a lot of bank security and ATM video, probably most of it of nothing, can you combine them and narrow it down to the bits where there's actual action at or near the ATM?"

A pause, then she said, "Yes, it is digital."

And again after a moment, "Yes, stationary camera right above the machine, and on each corner of the building."

A longer pause this time while she listened. And then she smiled. "Great."

She disconnected the call and put away the phone, then looked over at him. "He can isolate the area we want, and give us just the times when something happens or there's movement in that area. And we can watch it sped up a bit and still not miss anything."

"Perfect," Zach said. "That'll save hours."

It was still, they realized later, going to take hours; that ATM got a lot of traffic. The field of view of the three cameras covered the entire side of the bank from the curb at the street to the edge of the parking lot, the parking spots dedicated to the ATM, and the machine itself.

"You don't all have to do this," Zach said, but Bedford shook his head.

"More eyes the better," he said. "One person tends to zone out, and you miss stuff."

"Party," Sasha said. "Let's send out for pizza."

"Later," Zach said. "We're going to be here a while."

He started with a close-up of the girl, so they would all recognize her.

"We should go backward," Bedford said after they had all watched the young woman make the withdrawal from the Durbin account. "No sense watching it all from the beginning if we don't have to."

"Good idea," Zach agreed.

"This is slick," Sasha said as the playback began. She glanced at Reeve. "This computer geek of yours, how old is he?"

"I'm not sure. Mid-twenties, at a guess. Josh found him after he hacked into a supposedly secure system at Redstone Technologies."

"And hired him?" Sasha asked.

She nodded. "He's Redstone now, to the bone."

"Is he cute?"

Caught off guard, Reeve blinked. Then she smiled. "I don't know, I've never actually met him. He sounds cute, though."

"That's a start," Sasha said with a laugh.

How could somebody *sound* cute? Zach wondered. But he was too surprised by Sasha's interest to say anything; she'd never given any indication she was into computers. Or into those who were. Russ wasn't going to be happy, so it was probably a good thing he was out responding to another possible call for help from a worried parent.

"When we wind this up, I'll be going by to thank him for his help," Reeve told the girl. "Want to come?"

Sasha grinned. "I've never been to Redstone," she said.

"All the more reason," Reeve said, returning the girl's grin.

Zach exchanged a glance with Bedford, who rolled his eyes at the girl talk, but good-naturedly.

A couple of hours later, with the debris of delivery pizza and sodas spread around the room, they struck gold. The time stamp on the video showed four hours before the withdrawal when the same girl, same clothes, walked up to the machine. Again she came from the sidewalk, and again she looked around with obvious nervousness. And this time, somebody who also wanted to use the ATM came up behind her and stood waiting. It was enough to panic her, and she bolted.

"Run through it again," Bedford said.

Zach, who had taken over the controls while

Bedford ate his slice of pizza, backed up the video and played the aborted attempt again.

"She so does not want to be there," Sasha said.

Bedford's cell phone rang, and Zach hit Pause so he could answer. The man quickly wiped fingers greasy from the last slice of pizza and answered. He had a brief conversation that consisted mostly of him listening. When he hung up, he gave them all a resigned look.

"Well, now there's a surprise," he said. "That was Tigard. Seems our little barista turned ATM bandit walked off the job at the coffee place about a half hour after you guys left."

"We scared her into running," Zach said.

"For real. They contacted her roommate, who works nights and so was at their apartment. She said Stephanie—that's her name, Stephanie Moore—came home very agitated, threw some things into a duffel bag and took off. Said she'd be gone a while."

Sasha frowned. "She's our kidnapper? That doesn't seem right."

"No, it doesn't," Zach said.

"Maybe she just snagged his card," Sasha suggested.

"Then how'd she get his PIN number?" Zach asked.

"Charmed it out of him?" Bedford suggested. "She's pretty enough, and if he's the social maladroit he seems to be, he'd be susceptible...."

Zach nodded slowly. "Could be."

"I'll go catch up with Tigard and see what else they've got," Bedford said, already on his feet.

"Good. Sasha, can you go to the café and talk to the co-worker? She might be more forthcoming to you."

"Sure."

They did a lot of that, covering ground the police had already been over. But it was true that sometimes people were more willing to talk to somebody who wasn't a cop, and they often got things the cops couldn't.

After Sasha had gone, Reeve turned back to the monitor.

"Play that again, will you?" she asked.

Zach backed up the playback until Stephanie Moore was just visible coming into the frame.

"No, go back a little further."

He did. Reeve's gaze fastened on something. Zach looked, but didn't see anything unusual.

"Hold it," she said.

Zach hit the stop button.

"Back it up just a little."

He did as she asked.

"There," she said, and he stopped it again.

"What?" he asked.

She leaned forward, staring. "Can we zoom this?"

"Some," Zach said, "but the resolution goes down pretty quickly."

"Just a little, then. That lower-left corner."

He pushed two buttons in succession on the control. Reeve leaned forward a bit more, and Zach found himself following suit.

"There," she said, pointing. "See?"

He followed the direction of her slender finger.

He hadn't noticed before, he'd been so focused on the girl. But there, into the camera's field of view by a sliver, was the front of a car.

A red car. A familiar red car.

Zach's gaze shot to Reeve's face.

She wasn't surprised. In fact, she looked grim, as if she'd both expected and dreaded this.

"Damn," he murmured.

"Indeed."

She sounded exactly like she looked. Grim.

Chapter 13

"Maybe it's not. We can't really see enough of the car to be sure," Zach said.

"No, we can't."

Reeve understood his reaction. She'd hoped against hope she was wrong, for so many reasons.

"But you think it is."

"Yes."

"You've thought it before now."

"Yes."

Zach let out a low whistle. "Josh is not going to be happy."

"No. But he's not going to know yet, because right now I have nothing solid to go on. It's all circumstantial and gut feelings."

"And we'd better have all our ducks in a row before we tell him something like this."

She nodded. "He trusts us completely, but this…this is different."

"It's family."

"And he doesn't have much."

Zach gave the image on the screen, with the nose of that red car just visible in the corner, a last look. Then he clicked it off and put the control down on the table rather sharply.

"We still need to find him," he said.

"Yes," she said. "I want him in front of Josh, admitting everything."

"Whatever 'everything' is." Zach's tone was dry.

"Do we tell the others?"

He thought for a moment, then shook his head. "We still need to do what they're out there trying to do. Find the kid. That hasn't changed. Besides…"

"What if I'm wrong? Believe me, I'm very aware of the possibility."

She wished she wasn't. Before Scott Westin's death, she would have run with this. But now, she couldn't help doubting. Although it hadn't been her instincts about Scott that had been wrong, it was that they hadn't come soon enough.

"Those gut feelings…." he began, as if he'd read her thoughts.

"I've learned to trust them." And I'm trying to

trust them again, she added silently. "But in this case, it's not enough."

"Not enough to hurt Josh like this will hurt him." His voice was tight, strained, and Reeve knew just how he felt.

"Exactly."

Zach shook his head. "I don't get it. Josh has already given so much, done so much for this kid."

"Maybe too much. Maybe spoiled him, made him feel he had the right to more."

"More of a free ride? I don't get the mentality."

"I don't think anybody who doesn't have the mentality can understand it." She thought of Josh's long-standing policy on charity, how willing he was to help anybody who was trying to help themselves. "It's the difference between a handout and a hand up."

Zach was pacing now, and with surprise Reeve realized he was angry.

Very angry.

"Let's just find him," he said, sounding as grim now as she had looked. "We'll deal with him then."

"That's the plan," Reeve agreed. "We—"

She stopped as his cell rang. He grabbed it, glanced at the screen, said "Sasha," and answered.

A moment later he disconnected the call.

"Let's go," he said. "The other girl at the café was ticked enough at getting stuck working alone to tell Sasha that Stephanie had mentioned something about having gone to see that fancy new hotel at the beach last night."

Reeve grabbed her purse and followed. She knew where he meant; the Bluewater Hotel had been all over the news before it even existed. There had been a fight over zoning, construction, size and all the other things that seemed inevitable these days.

"Do we call Bedford or Detective Tigard?" she asked as he turned to lock the front door, since there was no one left in the building at the moment.

He gave her a curious look. "You're asking me?"

She shrugged. "This whole operation is your territory. It wouldn't exist if not for you. I'm just here to help and grease the wheels where I can. So yes, I'm asking you."

She looked up at him, waiting. And trying to decipher the odd look that had come into his eyes. It was a combination of speculation, calculation, resistance and acquiescence at the same time.

And heat.

She realized it a moment too late; his mouth was on hers.

She'd thought her memory had embroidered upon that first kiss. Thought it had just been so long since she'd allowed a man close enough to kiss her that she'd made it more than it had really been, had made it deeper, hotter, sweeter.

She hadn't.

If anything, her memory had blunted the effect, had quashed the reality of her body surging to life, pumping, heating, at the mere touch of this man's lips.

She didn't pull away. On some level that wasn't already engulfed by her body's response she realized that. And from there it was only another step to the knowledge that she *wanted* this. She wanted this, and she had for a long time. Longer than she really wanted to admit, perhaps from the moment she had seen the gentleness and caring this big, strong, tough-when-necessary man was capable of.

She couldn't think clearly. Nothing could gain a foothold against the incredible sensations his mouth was evoking.

And then she could no longer think at all. His tongue swept over her lips, testing, asking. She parted them without hesitation, wanting the taste of him closer, hotter, deeper. She felt his hands at the back of her head, cupping, holding so that he could probe further. She welcomed the sweet invasion, teasing his tongue with her own, her heart hammering at the unfamiliar yet welcome taste and feel of him.

The blare of a car horn from the street disrupted the moment. She nearly let out an audible protest as he lifted his head. She heard him take in a deep, harsh breath, as if he felt as short on oxygen as she did. He rested his forehead against hers, and she heard him swallow as if his throat were tight. And she was thankful for each sign that she hadn't been alone in that chaos of heat and racing heartbeats.

"Damn," he murmured, not in a tone of cursing but in one of wonder.

"Wow," she said, feeling some acknowledgement was necessary.

His head lifted. She felt the touch of his finger under her chin as he urged her to look at him. She was strangely hesitant, almost afraid of what she would see in his face. What she saw was a reflection of her own tangled feelings, and that somehow eased her tension.

"Reeve—"

He stopped when she shook her head. "Not now," she said. "We have to go."

His mouth—that amazing, wonderful mouth—tightened, but after a moment he nodded. "Later, then."

Later. It was as much promise as agreement, she realized as they got into his car. She was glad of the reprieve, however; she needed to think about this.

But in the meantime, they had a job to do. With an effort, she repeated the question that had somehow started this.

"Call the police?"

He gave her a sideways look that acknowledged the side road they'd just taken before he answered with a shake of his head. "Let's make sure he's there first. We try to save the police as much leg-work as we can."

She nodded her understanding. She looked out the window as they headed toward the Pacific. It wasn't long before she could see the glint of it in the sunlight. It looked as it had the first time she'd seen it as a child, blue and endless to the horizon, there only by the miracle of gravity, a concept her young mind had struggled to comprehend.

And the miracle of a kiss? Can you comprehend that?

She cringed inwardly at the thought. Because she didn't know the answer. And if she couldn't comprehend, could she simply accept? Accept the truth that had just been seared into her consciousness, that this man had an effect on her like no other? That this man, the man she had shared so much with, so much emotion, so much pain, was the one who stirred her so, the one who could get her past that pain?

That he had his own pain to get past, and that it stemmed from the identical source, was an irony she couldn't even wrap her mind around right now.

With an effort born of hours of intensive training and the unyielding demands of Draven, she forced her mind back to the task at hand.

As Zach had said, later.

It was almost too easy, Zach thought. Once they'd gotten past the busy clerks to management, the Redstone name—one of the main pillars of the hospitality industry, with Redstone Resorts the envy of hoteliers around the world—got them the rest of the way.

"Checking out the competition?" the registration desk manager had asked with a nervous chuckle. A small, wiry man with dark-framed glasses, wearing a hotel blazer in a rather unfortunate shade of yellow, Mr. L. Litner looked a bit like a bee, and buzzed about in a fashion that carried on the resemblance.

"I suspected as much when young Mr. Redstone checked in. Unless he's checking us out for a possible purchase?"

Zach ignored the query. "Young Mr. Redstone?"

"I meant no insult, of course. But he does look rather young."

"Is this who you mean?" Reeve pulled out the photograph of Rod and held it out to the man.

"Yes, that's him."

"And he checked in under the name of Redstone?"

Puzzled, and a bit worried now, the man nodded. "Rodney Redstone. I remember because of the alliteration." He gestured at his own name tag with its two Ls. "I tend to notice."

"Do you check ID?" Reeve asked.

"Well, no," the man said, sounding a bit uncomfortable. "Wouldn't be very welcoming, would it? But he did have a credit card."

"In the name Redstone?" Zach asked.

"I believe so. Let me go check…"

He left the office so quickly it was obvious he was nervous about this whole thing.

"He used the debit card?" Reeve said. "Now that's stupid."

"They put it through like a credit card charge, so it takes a bit longer. But yes, he should have used cash from the ATM," Zach agreed.

The manager was back quickly, a printout of a registration in his hand.

"Yes, here it is," the man said. "He used a credit card in the name of Joshua Redstone." The man looked up. "That's *the* Mr. Redstone, isn't it?"

"Yes, it is," Reeve said, her voice tight. She was apparently upset enough to drop her pen, which bounced a couple of feet and landed at the bee's feet. "Sorry," she said as she went over and bent to pick it up.

"The clerk who checked him in said that he said he was a relative of Mr. Redstone's, not Mr. Redstone himself," the man said.

"He is," Zach said. "Unfortunately. We need to talk to him immediately."

"Oh, I'm afraid I can't give you his room number. That's against policy."

"Look, this kid is involved in—"

"That's all right, Mr. Litner," Reeve said smoothly, cutting Zach off. "We understand, and would never ask you to violate hotel policy. Redstone's in the same business, after all."

"Thank you," the man said gratefully.

To his credit, Zach didn't argue as she ushered him out of the man's office. He didn't speak until they were back out in the hotel lobby and clear of anyone within earshot.

"I presume there was a reason for the retreat?"

"Room 407."

He blinked. "What?"

"He's in room 407."

The image of her dropping the pen literally at Litner's feet and having to go pick it up ran through his head. And a grin spread across his face.

"Slick," he said. "Very, very slick."

"Now," she said, "we need a fruit basket. Or flowers. Something."

He was with her now. "Something to deliver, you mean?"

She nodded. "I'll do it. You stay just out of sight. He'll be more likely to open the door to a woman."

They headed for the small gift shop to see what could be had. A ridiculously overpriced floral arrangement later, they were on their way to the elevator.

He had to admire the smooth patter she came up with when Rod—clearly alive and quite well—opened the door. He wanted to slap the kid silly, but she rattled off a gushing stream of flattery aimed at the phony Redstone as if he were the real thing, saying the flowers were a gesture of welcome from the hotel to their esteemed guest. Rod ate it up—and stepped back to let her in.

Zach moved quickly then, stepping in after her and closing the door behind him. Rod was a little slow on the uptake; he just looked puzzled.

"Let me formally introduce myself," Reeve said after she'd set the flowers down on the dresser and turned to face Rod. She took out a small wallet and flipped it open to show an ID card in the Redstone colors of red and gray, displaying the distinctive Redstone logo of the Hawk jet, the plane that had built an empire.

"I'm Reeve Fox. Redstone Security."

Rod went pale. The smug expression vanished, as did the swagger. Zach had to admit, the announcement that she was Redstone Security had a much bigger effect than he ever could have had. Rod obviously knew their reputation, knew this was second only to being caught by the cops.

Rod glanced at Zach. "Who are you?"

The wobble in his voice made it clear he was afraid of the answer, and Zach guessed he probably thought he was a cop. For a moment, Zach almost wished he was right.

"This," Reeve said before he could answer, "is the head of the Westin Foundation, a man who has wasted a great deal of time and resources looking for you, resources that could have been much better spent helping people who really needed it than being wasted on your childish little game."

"It wasn't a game!"

"No, it wasn't." Zach spoke for the first time. Anger had been building in him from the moment Rod had opened the door and they'd seen he was all right, and that it all truly had been a scam. "It was extortion."

"That it was," Reeve said. "And I believe that'll get you a felony conviction and seven years in prison."

"Hey!" Rod yelped in protest.

"You're old enough to be tried as an adult," Zach said, keeping his temper with an effort. "Welcome to the land of personal responsibility."

"My uncle will never press charges," Rod said defiantly. "I'm the only nephew he's got. He'll just be glad I'm not dead."

Something snapped inside Zach, so sharply he was surprised it wasn't audible. He took one big step forward and backed Rod against a wall.

"You useless little piece of crap," he hissed out. "You're nothing but a leech, a parasite, trying to suck the life out of a man who's worth a hundred of you. He'd do anything for you, if you just showed him one iota of effort to help yourself. But no, you have to cheat, to try and steal it, to have it handed to you with no effort on your part. The world owes you a living, is that what you think?"

"Zach."

He barely heard Reeve say his name. He couldn't stop now, it was beyond stopping, beyond his ability to control. A dam had broken, and everything he'd buried for the past year was pouring out.

"It makes me sick," he said, ignoring the fear growing in Rod's face as he cowered before the onslaught. "Sick that you'd try this against Josh of all people. You'd have *nothing* if it wasn't for him. If it wasn't for all he's already done for you, you'd really have something to whine about."

"Zach!"

He felt her hand on his arm. Felt it, tried to pull back, but it was like a storm was upon him, and he could do nothing but finish it.

"You make me sick, that you're here and alive, utterly worthless, while better people aren't. How can you be here, and Scotty…Scotty…"

She was holding him. She had her arms around him, squeezing, hanging on as if she were trying to quell the storm with her grip, with her body. He gulped in air, closed his eyes, fought it. Her arms tightened, and in her fierce hanging on, she somehow gave him something to grab onto himself

He half turned toward her. Unsteadily. He barely heard Rodney whine, "He's crazy, get him off me."

"Shut up," Reeve said sharply to the boy. "You deserve every word he said and more." Then, to him, "It's you I'm worried about, Zach. He's not worth your pain."

An odd weakness flooded over him. He staggered back a half step, felt as if he were going to fall. But she was there, holding him, propping him up.

Just as she had a year ago.

"It's okay, Zach," she whispered.

Okay. Okay as in all right? It wasn't all right. It would never, ever be all right again. He knew that. But okay wasn't the same, was it? Everything didn't have to be all right to be okay.

And here and now, with her arms around him and her voice soft in his ear, for the first time in a year he thought deep down he just might be okay.

Chapter 14

"Weird. He was so smart about some things, but so dumb about others."

Zach made the comment as they continued to search the hotel room. Reeve wasn't sure what she was looking for, just that she was trained to be thorough and if there was evidence of any further manipulations on Rod's part she wanted to know about them now. But there didn't seem to be anything; apparently Rod had only checked in this morning.

They hadn't told the hotel that the room had been vacated, they didn't trust someone on the staff not to find a reporter who might be interested in a bit of scandal connected to the Redstone name.

They'd managed to keep the "kidnapping" out of the bloodthirsty media so far, and now that it had degenerated into this morass of personal greed and entitlement, that was even more important.

"Maybe he was trying to impress the girl," Reeve said as she pulled open a nightstand drawer, the last place she hadn't looked. "Maybe he promised her this in return for helping him with the ATM withdrawal."

"Men will do that," Zach said neutrally. "But she's not here."

"He was planning on it," she said. "Maybe she backed out on him."

He looked over his shoulder at her as she lifted a brand-new, unopened box of condoms from the drawer.

Zach grimaced. "I don't know whether to feel disgusted or glad he was planning safe sex. It never ceases to amaze me how birds of a feather find each other."

"The smell," Reeve said. Zach blinked. "Rod smelled what he thought was a ripe plum for the picking. He talked about it, and waited for somebody else to respond to the smell."

"Is that a Draven analogy?" he asked.

She laughed. "Of course."

"Somehow that doesn't surprise me," he said.

She tossed the box on the bed.

"I hope," she said, "that the cops are scaring the daylights out of him."

"I'm sure they are. They don't take something like this lightly." He sat down on the edge of the bed. "Do you think Josh will bail him out?"

"I hope not," she said fervently. "That's what got him into this. I mean, I understand why he feels responsible for the kid, but this is way over the line."

"So you think he should jettison Rod?"

There was something in his tone that made her realize it wasn't just a casual question. She sat down beside him.

"I think," she said carefully, "that it's time to look at the big picture with Rod. The long-term picture. He's screwed up in a big way, and he needs to learn that. And saving him from the consequences of his actions yet again is not going to help."

"Tough love?"

"Something like that, yes. This may be the last chance for him to turn into something other than… everything you called him."

Zach grimaced. "I was…out of control."

"I know. And I understand."

He gave her a sideways look. "I think…I think maybe you do. More than anyone."

That warmed her more than she thought words ever could. She smiled at him, but the old ache about Scotty, and knowing that they both would feel it forever, made it a pained one.

As if he could sense the feelings behind the smile

he reached out. She went into his arms as if it were second nature, and for a long time they simply sat there, clinging, as if combining their pain somehow eased it for both of them.

And then it changed, altered to something else. Reeve felt the shift, felt the warmth of friendship turn to something hotter, something bigger, something…inevitable.

She looked up, wanting to see his face, his eyes. When he took it as an offering of her mouth and kissed her, she realized she'd wanted that, too.

With the pressure of finding Rod gone now, nothing seemed to be in their way. And Reeve realized with a little shock that she'd been waiting for this time, waiting for them to be free to explore what had been growing between them.

It was a long, leisurely kiss, marking how things had changed, that there was no rush now, nothing hanging over them that had to be dealt with, no interruptions bound to happen. But it was just as hot, and Reeve's senses reacted just as quickly to the touch, the feel of him.

He deepened the kiss, exploring, probing, and she welcomed him, her fingers clutching his shoulders, tightening as the flood of sensations swept through her.

She was nearly lost in the flow when he stopped. The sudden chill of his absence drew a tiny sound of protest from her.

"Reeve," he said, his voice thick. "I don't think—"

He stopped, swallowing audibly.

"Not thinking sounds like the right approach," she said, wanting him back, kissing her again.

"No, I meant…I don't think…here."

It took her a moment to process, the heat of his kiss being slow to fade.

"Here?"

"I know, we've got a bed, condoms…but not here."

She felt a spurt of relief; she'd thought he wanted to call off the whole thing.

"The scene of the crime, as it were?" she asked softly.

"Exactly," he said, sounding relieved that she'd understood.

"But…somewhere?"

She saw his eyes change as he looked at her, saw them widen, then narrow. "Oh, yes. Somewhere."

She let out a long breath. Regretfully, she said, "We should see Josh anyway."

He sounded like she felt when he agreed. "Yes. I know."

So it was with that *somewhere* thought hovering that they headed to Redstone headquarters. Zach drove while Reeve called ahead; it was past the end of the work day for most people, but they both knew

Josh wasn't most people. When she'd called to report they'd found Rod, St. John had answered. This time it was Josh himself. Reeve told him only that they were on their way to report; the truth of this nasty affair wasn't something she wanted to tell him on the phone.

She didn't want to tell him at all, but she knew Josh wasn't one to hide from the truth, no matter how painful.

Neither was Zach, she thought as she glanced at him after she'd disconnected. He might bury his emotions about the truth, but he faced it, head-on. He'd turned his grief into something positive, and had ended up more whole than she had. She felt a flash of shame at how she'd let herself wallow in it for so long. But no more.

No more.

"I haven't been here in a while," Zach said as they parked outside the ten-story building that was the heart of Redstone.

It looked much like any other office building in this light-industrial zone. On the outside, anyway. It was only when you got inside that you realized how different it was. Built around a big, lush garden that included a pond and a waterfall that gave off soothing, mellow sounds, Redstone headquarters was one of a kind as far as office buildings went. Each section of the building was devoted to one aspect of the empire Josh Redstone had built: aviation, technology, Redstone Resorts, and Research and Development. The only notable absence was Redstone Security; by necessity they were off site and unknown by face to most of the Redstone staff.

Each section of the building was open on the inner edge to the garden, letting the cool peace of it become part of their workaday world. In the heat of a California summer, the garden was a favorite spot for all of Redstone, and some of the best thinking and greatest ideas came out of that halcyon spot. Zach had retreated there more than once himself when he'd worked in this building.

Josh's office was on the top floor, as one might expect, but not for the reasons most CEOs' offices were. Josh was up there because most of the building was devoted to the work of Redstone, and for him, that was the heart and soul of it, not some tower office.

It also fit his daily routine; Josh didn't simply come to work and disappear into his office every day, he made a point of working his way up to the top floor by traveling through every department, greeting everyone in each, most by name, and opening himself to questions or concerns. Everybody at Redstone knew Josh's door was always open to them, but he went a step beyond, and made himself accessible on a daily basis when he was here. Anyone who worked for him could take him aside on those morning tours and talk to him about anything, and they all knew it. As a consequence, it actually rarely happened, but when it did, it was usually something worth hearing.

It had been on one of those tours that Zach had approached Josh and told him he didn't think he could go back to his old job, to his day-to-day work. And to his surprise, Josh told him he'd been expecting this, and to come to his office.

And there he'd laid it all out for him, the plan for the Scott Westin Foundation, funded by Redstone and with the sole function of finding missing children. He'd given Zach free rein to build his own staff, his own way of working, and to find a way to fill the gap between what the understaffed police could do and what should be done.

And now, Zach thought, here he was, about to blast the man he admired and respected beyond all others out of the water.

"I wonder if he's going to start Redstone Ship Building," Reeve said as they entered the building and headed to the security checkpoint; Ian Gamble's scanning system was quick and as foolproof as any such system could be, and they'd be through it in short order.

"That was quite a boat," Zach said. And finding you aboard was quite a shock.

He glanced at her as she put her palm against the hand scanner and looked directly into the retinal scanner. Just the memory of how close they'd come in that hotel room had the power to rattle him, to shift his pulse into high gear. It had been a long time since he'd felt anything like that. In fact, he wasn't sure he ever had before.

Idiot, he told himself. Why the hell did you stop? That has to be the stupidest thing you've ever done.

He stepped up to the scanners himself, not thinking about what he was doing. The only thing he could seem to hold on to was the hope that she wasn't going to change her mind.

As was typical, Josh opened the door to his office himself; no one ran interference for him here. The guard dogs were downstairs; here he was with family, and he didn't feel it necessary.

Josh's office hadn't changed since the last time Zach had been there. Compared to those of others of his status—although Zach knew there weren't many—it was beyond unpretentious. The furnishings were of high quality, with the warmth of polished oak and the soft plush of nubuck leather, but they were chosen for comfort and function, not show.

Josh indicated one of the leather sofas, then bent his lanky frame to take a seat on the other. Zach glanced at Reeve; they hadn't talked about who would make this unpleasant report, he as head of the Westin Foundation, or she as the representative of Redstone Security.

As it turned out, neither of them had too.

"It was Rod, wasn't it?" Josh asked softly.

Zach met Reeve's glance briefly. She spoke before he had the chance.

"Yes, sir, I'm afraid so."

Josh sighed heavily. For a moment his gray eyes closed, and he looked older than his forty-four years. Then he straightened and looked at them both.

"I suspected as much," he said.

Zach and Reeve exchanged glances.

"I was almost certain when I got the e-mail, to that address. I suppose he was afraid I'd recognize his voice if he called." Josh shook his head. "But I wanted to give him the benefit of the doubt, and I didn't want my suspicions to affect your investigation."

"We understand," Zach said. "You had to be sure."

"Still, I'm sorry to have put you both through this."

"You couldn't risk ignoring the possibility that it was real, Josh," Reeve said gently.

"No, I couldn't." For a moment a deep, searing pain flickered in his eyes. Zach felt a tightening in his chest for this man who'd done so much for him, and others.

Reeve offered to give him the details, but Josh shook his head. "Just send me the report," he said. "I'll read it…later."

"What are you going to do?" Reeve ask, her voice sounding like Zach felt, aching for Josh's pain.

"I don't know yet."

He got to his feet, and they did the same. He thanked them both again. That was clearly all he wanted to hear for now, and Zach felt a sense of relief. He and Reeve were headed for the door when Josh asked Reeve to stay for a moment.

She didn't look surprised, merely told Zach she'd meet him down at the car. Reluctantly he left her there, then chided himself for having a one-track mind, unable to think about anything except keeping his suddenly reawakened body in check.

"Mad at me?"

Reeve didn't pretend to misunderstand Josh's question.

"Because you set me up?"

He grimaced, but didn't deny it. "Yes."

Reeve's mouth quirked. As usual, Josh had known what he was doing. He'd known what she needed before she had, and had made sure she had no choice but to do it. He'd set her up, but she couldn't seem to mind.

"No. I never was, really. Just...afraid I couldn't handle it."

"But you did."

"Yes. I had no choice."

"Reeve, I didn't mean to—"

He stopped when she held up a hand. She wondered for an instant how many people on the outside could do that with a boss as high-powered as Josh Redstone, and took it as a testament to the man that any member of the Redstone family could and would if they felt they had to.

"Not you. Zach. He gave me no choice. How could I not go on, not get back in the saddle as it were, after watching him? What he's done is nothing less than amazing."

"Yes, it is," Josh agreed, acknowledgment and something else, something more personal, glinting in his eyes. "He is."

"Yes." Reeve couldn't deny it. Didn't want to.

"Are you…back?" Josh asked.

She didn't even have to think about it. "Yes."

He nodded, a gesture of finality. "Good."

She turned to go, but at the door stopped and looked back. "Thank you."

He grinned at her then, that easy, lopsided grin that fooled so many into thinking he was less than he was, that tool that had helped him get where he was.

"You're welcome, darlin'," he drawled exaggeratedly.

Reeve was laughing as she left, feeling more lighthearted than she could remember in a very long time.

Zach was standing beside his car, talking on his

cell phone. As she got closer she realized he was talking to Bedford. He disconnected just as she reached him.

"Josh should just toss that kid to the wolves," Zach said grimly. "Let him see how the adult world deals with extortionists."

"I doubt he will," Reeve said. "But I think he'll let him stew for a good long while."

"I hope so."

They got into the car, and Zach started the motor. "I really understand why Josh rarely trusts anyone. He can't."

Reeve nodded. "If it were me, I don't know if I would be able to trust anybody who hadn't come up with me, who knew me before the money came."

He nodded in agreement, then lapsed into silence. They sat there, the car running, for a long, quiet moment. Then, in a voice oddly hoarse, Zach asked, "Where to?"

Reeve looked at him, saw the look on his face. And the heat she'd banked since they'd left the hotel roared to life within her.

"Oh….somewhere," she said, the sudden tightness in her throat making her voice husky.

He let out a compressed breath and muttered something that sounded like thanks.

Somewhere turned out to be her little house, mainly because it was closer, although Zach admitted wryly his apartment was only where he lived, not a home. Reeve remembered the large, nice house he'd had before, and assumed it had gone in the divorce from Deborah.

That made her remember all he'd been through, which triggered her sometimes annoying sense of fairness. It was nearly swamped by the passion that rose anew so quickly it had them clawing at each other's clothes, dropping a jacket, a shirt, a blouse, and kicking off shoes as they neared her bedroom.

It was all she could do to back a half step away from him and ask breathlessly, "Are you sure about this?"

"Isn't that supposed to be my question?"

He sounded wryly amused. Or nervous, she wasn't sure which.

"And is this really the time to have second thoughts?" he asked, indicating their half-naked state and his own fierce arousal.

"Better now than…later."

"There is that," he agreed, somewhat fervently.

Then he reached out and cupped her face in his hands. When he spoke, his voice was quiet and deadly serious.

"I'm not whole, Reeve. You know that, don't you? I don't think I ever will be again. But you…you make me feel like I can go on anyway."

As a declaration of feeling perhaps it wouldn't be enough for most women. But for Reeve, who knew better than anyone what it had had to triumph over, it was nothing less than remarkable.

"That's enough," she whispered. "More than enough."

He let out a low, harsh groan as he reached for her. The heat of his bare skin on hers made the fire that had only been banked inside her flare anew, rising to engulf her with the return of his lips to hers. He trailed kisses over her cheek, down the side of her neck to her shoulder, and then, with exquisite care to the swell of her breast above the lace trim of her bra.

She moaned at the intimate touch. She wanted him naked, now. She wanted to be naked with him, now. She wanted to touch him, feel him, caress the rigid column of flesh he was offering her. She wanted it all, and she wanted it right now, as fast as she could get it.

"Yes," he rasped out, his voice nearly hoarse, and she realized she'd voiced her wants. "We'll go slow…next time."

And he gave her what she wanted. He stripped off the last of his clothes and then hers, and took her down to the bed with an urgency that fired her even higher. She went still for a moment when his fingers found the nasty scar on her left side, the badge of a precious life saved. But he bent and kissed it, acknowledging and saluting the painful history at the same time.

And then he was touching her, kissing her, everywhere, with an almost frantic energy that drove her mad, until she could not hold still any longer. She clawed at him, urged him on with wordless sounds and the arch of her body. He shifted over her, slipped between her legs. She felt the blunt probe, reached for him, guided him, and cried out with shocked pleasure as he slammed home into her welcoming heat.

He called her name, and it was the most thrilling thing she'd ever heard. She'd never felt anything like this, never known such wild, mindless insanity. He was bracing her with his hands and he plunged deep, but it still wasn't enough and she lifted her hips to meet him, to take him harder and deeper. It was like another dam breaking, this time in them both, and the breach unleashed a madness that blotted out the rest of the world.

He rolled, taking her with him until she was on top, straddling him.

"Zach!" His name burst from her as his hands came up to her breasts.

"Ride me," he gasped out. "Hard."

The image his words brought to her mind nearly sent her over the edge. She rocked on him, arching her back to drive him deeper, crying out as he filled her to exquisite tightness. Her head lolled back as she felt her body gather under his touch. His fingers tugged at her nipples, sending darts of fire through her to pool at the place they were joined. And then he was touching her there, stroking, circling.

Her body clenched violently, and she cried out his name again. His hands went to her hips and he slammed her down hard against him. She felt him swell even harder within her. He bucked upward, once, twice, and then she was gone, driven by his body into a fiery, wild place she'd never been before, the sound of his husky groan the only thing anchoring her to this world.

Chapter 15

Reeve had not had many "morning afters" to deal with. And as she lay there in the dim light of dawn, savoring the unexpectedly sweet warmth of Zach asleep beside her, she realized that the night befores hadn't been much to prize, either.

But this....

She wanted to reach for him again, but she had already awakened him once—as he had her, to be fair—and she was a little embarrassed at how...hungry she was.

She was also wary about that approaching morning. Would it be awkward, difficult? Or would they slide into it easily, just as they had slid into working together again? Would he withdraw, wish they hadn't, want to run now that the initial passion had been served?

Zachary Westin doesn't run.

She'd missed that little voice, she thought. Missed the instincts that brought it on. Instincts that were apparently back and working at full power. And, as usual, right.

Zach wouldn't run. It just wasn't in him. There'd be no game-playing, no "I'll call you," tossed out casually and meant just as casually. He would—

The faint musical call of her cell phone from the other room interrupted her speculations. She got up quickly, hoping it wouldn't wake him; she wouldn't have heard it herself if she hadn't already been awake.

She wasn't surprised at the early call when she saw who it was; St. John did what he did when he did it, and didn't worry much about it being convenient for anybody else. He expected the same sort of dedication to Redstone from everyone else that he himself had, and he therefore never apologized, either.

She answered quickly, before it could ring again.

"Fox."

"Fax on?"

"Yes."

"Sending. Scrambled."

She knew what that meant; whatever he was sending, he'd probably acquired by less-than-straightforward means. Nobody questioned St.

John's methods, because his results were so amazing. Of course, just the fact that he was faxing it over a landline instead of simply e-mailing it to her told her it was sensitive material.

"Fox?" A pause then, uncharacteristic enough to make her wonder what was up with the man. "He's not going to like it."

She didn't have to ask what "he" St. John meant. In fact, if he knew that she and Zach had spent the entire night exploring each other into exhaustion, she wouldn't be the least surprised. Embarrassed, but not surprised.

"Thanks for the heads-up," she said, cringing inwardly as she assessed how bad it had to be to stir St. John to that warning.

"I'll be in touch."

She knew that meant he was still following a trail. St. John wasn't one to give up before the job was actually done.

After the man had hung up with his characteristic abruptness, she walked into the small second bedroom that served as her office. The dedicated fax machine was already humming. She checked the paper supply, then simply stood waiting, wondering what bombshell was about to arrive in the output tray.

Moments later she stood there with what was indeed a bombshell in her hands. After her first quick scan she went back and started to read. St.

John hadn't included any observations of his own, but then, he didn't have to; the pages pretty much spoke for themselves. And what they said was going to wreak havoc on Zach's world all over again.

And I have to do it. Again.

The thought of what this knowledge would do to him wiped away any bit of self-pity she felt that once more she would be the one who had to deliver the blow. She'd made a vow never to let herself get so lost in that vicious pool again. Her focus now had to be Zach, and getting him through this. She wanted what they had, what they could build together, to survive this, and that was going to take some doing given what she now had to do.

As if her thoughts had summoned him, he was in the doorway to her office.

"Early start."

She froze for an instant, wishing she'd had more time to figure out how to do this, but knowing she couldn't delay. Not this.

"Yes," she said. "Afraid so."

"Something new?"

She took in a deep breath before saying carefully, "Not exactly. Something new about…something old."

He frowned, then yawned; clearly he was feeling as she had before the contents of St. John's fax had slammed her completely awake.

"Come on, I'll fix coffee," she said, turning to head for the kitchen. She'd stall him until he was awake, at least, she added silently.

He stopped her as she passed him with a hand on her shoulder. She looked up. He smiled.

Her mind scrambled to memorize that look, to sear how he looked at this moment in her mind, because she knew it wasn't going to last.

And then he kissed her, not with the heat of last night, but soft and sweet and somehow reassuring. When he released her she reached up and touched his face, tried to smile back. And the first hint of trouble appeared in his expression, as if he could sense that her smile was forced.

But he followed her to the kitchen, and stood by as she got the coffee machine up and going. She'd set the papers down within reach, keeping herself between them and Zach. She doubted he would ask as long as he thought they were related to some other Redstone case, but once he knew the truth there would be no stopping him.

Once he had half a mug of coffee in him and was obviously awake, she braced herself and took the plunge.

"Look at these."

He looked at the stack of papers she held, brows furrowed. "Me?"

She nodded. She wanted to warn him but she couldn't. He had to see it for himself, to follow the trail and arrive at the same place on his own. With an effort that belied the light weight of the stack of papers, she handed the faxed file to him, holding back only the last three pages.

He took them. Sat down on the stool pulled up to the eating bar at the end of the kitchen counter. Started to read. She saw the disgust come over his face as went from page to page of the police report on another child molestation and murder. When he'd finished, he tossed them down on the counter.

"By now I've read dozens of reports on pedophiles like that," he said tightly. "Especially unsolved ones."

"I know."

"It never ceases to amaze me how twisted and purely evil some people can be."

"Yes," Reeve said, her throat tight. She reached out and picked up the papers he'd read. She noticed with an odd detachment that her hand was trembling slightly. And then she set two more pages in front of him, side by side, so he could see them both at once.

She waited. Saw his brows furrow in puzzlement and knew it was time.

"The first page," she said quietly, "is a copy of the lease agreement of your former next-door neighbor. The middle initial E. stands for Edward."

His head came up, as if seeking her point.

"One nickname for Edward is—"

"Ned," he said tightly as realization hit. "He was the guy Deborah had the affair with?"

She nodded.

Zach let out a short, sharp breath. "The wife and the guy next door. What a cliché."

As she'd expected, he hadn't quite made the leap yet. He was still grappling with the details of his then-wife's affair.

"So I'm the butt of a bad lawyer joke," he said wryly.

She waited. Waited until he shook off the knowledge, which happened quickly enough to tell her he wasn't all that disturbed over Deborah's affair. At least, not any more. And that soothed Reeve's troubled spirit a little.

"He wasn't really a lawyer. If he had been, this would have been over sooner."

Zach frowned in puzzlement. Reeve gestured at the last page she'd given him. He looked at it, and his forehead creased again. "A fingerprint? The pedophile's?"

"Yes. They found it at the crime scene, but were never able to match it to anyone in the automated fingerprint ID system."

He looked up at her. Waiting. And she did it.

"The original lease was still in evidence. It had prints on it they were able to recover even after a year. One full thumb and a partial index finger. They ran them through AFIS."

She put the last, damning page she'd held back on top of the file, then set the whole stack in front of him again.

"They matched, Zach. The fingerprint on this unsolved case belonged to the man who signed the lease." The pedophile next door, Reeve thought grimly.

"My God," he whispered.

He'd gone pale. And Reeve knew he understood he was looking at the fingerprints of the man who had murdered his son.

Chapter 16

"But he was gone," Zach whispered. "He left months before Scotty..."

"I know," Reeve said. "He was careful. And patient. He left, stayed away long enough to remove himself from the immediate suspect pool, made sure nobody knew where he'd gone."

"And then he came back?"

"That's my guess."

"Where is he now?" he asked, his voice vibrating with tension.

"We don't know. But we've told the police, and they're looking. And now that we have his name—or at least one he's used, although Draven thinks it's likely he's arrogant enough to use his real name—and some prints, Draven and St. John are looking."

She knew he would understand what it meant to have the head of Redstone Security and Josh's own right-hand man on the hunt. He sat for a long time, looking down at the papers before him. But Reeve suspected he wasn't really seeing them at all. He was processing, with a brain likely shocked into near numbness, working his way through all the ramifications.

And finally, he got to the one she'd been dreading.

"She did this," he said, in a voice she'd never heard from him before. "She brought this garbage into our lives, gave him access to Scotty...."

Ned especially loved Scotty, too, and he wanted us all to be together....

She knew he'd remembered what Deborah had said. Knew it was all hitting him now. She tried to give him a distraction by returning to her earlier statement.

"He wasn't a real lawyer. If he had been, his fingerprints would have been taken for the bar. But he knew enough to carry off the facade of being one. He faked credentials, used those to have business cards printed up or did it himself, and he was set to go. Once the owner of the house saw all that, he didn't hesitate to rent to him."

"And Deborah didn't hesitate to have an affair with him."

"Zach," Reeve began, then paused, wondering

how she'd gotten into the position of defending his ex-wife. But it was the truth, and she had to say it. "She couldn't have known. There's no excuse for the affair, that's true, but she couldn't have known when she began it that he was a pedophile."

"But later…"

"Maybe. Maybe by the time any clues were there, she was too involved to see."

He looked up at her then. "You're defending her?"

"I'm trying to be fair."

Zach snapped out something alliterative about "fair," the curse made more effective by the fact that she'd never heard him use it before. He stood up so quickly the stool he'd been sitting on tipped over. The crash as it hit the floor, and the fact that Zach ignored it and headed for the door warned Reeve she had a lit powder keg on her hands.

"Zach!"

He didn't stop. She hadn't expected him to; a year of grief and anger and turmoil were coming to a head. She grabbed up the papers he'd left on the counter and raced after him. Pausing to lock her door, she didn't catch up to him until he was at his car. She didn't bother to try and talk him down now, he was too revved and too hot. She simply kept moving and grabbed his keys right out of his hand as she passed, stopping only when she was safely out of reach.

"Damn it, give me those."

"No. You're not driving anywhere."

"Give me the keys, Reeve."

"No. You have every right to be beyond furious, Zachary, but I won't have you end up in jail."

He started to speak, bit it back, and Reeve had the feeling she was glad he hadn't said whatever it was.

"I'll drive." He drew back slightly; he hadn't expected that. "What did you think, that I expected you not to confront her, to just walk away?"

Something changed in his expression then, something softer flickered in his eyes.

"Drive," was all he said, and he walked around to the passenger side.

Reeve was a little surprised when they pulled up at the new, luxurious-looking condo building he directed her to. She'd assumed they'd sold the house and split the proceeds, but she didn't think they could have gotten enough so that half would buy one of these lavish units.

"Nice place," she said as they got out and went into the lobby.

"She traded the house for it," Zach said.

"What about your half?" she asked as they stopped in front of the elevators and Zach hit the up button.

He shrugged. "I didn't want anything from that place."

She blinked. "So you let her take all of it?"

His jaw tightened. "I thought she deserved it. She was so devastated, and I—"

The arrival of the elevator—or perhaps the realization of how wrong he'd been—cut off his words. They stepped in, the doors closed. Zach reached for the number four button. Reeve stopped him.

"I'm going to stay out of this, Zach," she said. "Except that I'm not going to let it get physical."

He gave her a sideways look. "You think I'm going to kill her?"

"I think," she said carefully, "that once she faces the truth, killing her would be a mercy she doesn't deserve."

He went very still. His eyes went unfocused, as if he were looking inward. When he said, in a voice barely above a whisper, "Yes, it would," Reeve knew he was remembering his own nights of agony, and realizing how it would feel if he learned that someone he had brought into Scott's life had done this to him.

Deborah must not have looked through the peephole in the door, because when she opened it and saw Zach, she was clearly shocked.

"What are you doing here?"

"We're going to talk. And you're going to answer some questions."

"How dare you talk to me like that!"

She moved to slam the door. Zach stopped the door with a quick movement of his arm. Before Reeve quite realized how it had happened, they were inside.

"I'll call the police!"

Zach ignored her continued angry exclamations. "I may be calling them myself before we're through." His voice was quietly grim next to Deborah's shrillness.

Something about his demeanor must have gotten through to her, because she turned her attention to Reeve. Before she could open her mouth, Reeve held up her hands to stop her.

"I'm just here to keep the peace." She glanced at Zach. "Relatively, anyway."

Deborah turned back to Zach. "What gives you the right to storm into my home like this?"

"This," Zach hissed out, shoving the file at her.

"What is this?"

"It's documentation on a pedophile. The sick, twisted man who murdered my son."

She gasped, sank down on the small bench in the entryway. "They found him?"

"No, Deborah. You did."

He slapped the last page he had, the copy of the fake business card, on top of the damning fingerprint match she held. She looked at it, frowned, then went sickly pale.

"No," she whispered. "No."

Something clutched at Reeve's gut, making her faintly nauseous. She'd spent her Redstone career doing jobs that required her to be able to read people. She was good at it. Right most of the time.

Deborah Westin wasn't surprised.

She was shocked, even devastated, but she wasn't surprised. On some level, she'd known. Reeve could only hope Zach was too caught up in his own pain and anger to realize it, or she really might have to stop him from killing the woman where she sat.

She'd underestimated him.

"You knew," he said, his voice rising for the first time. "Damn you, you knew!"

Deborah was crying now. "No, Zach, no. I didn't know, not for sure. And not…not when we were together."

"But you suspected."

"I…wondered. He seemed to take to Scott so fast."

Zach swore, so full of pain it was agony to hear.

"Zach, please, understand. I was so unhappy—"

"And Scotty was a child. Who trusted you to keep him safe."

She was weeping steadily now. "Do you think I don't know that? I've been living with the fear of this day for a year."

"Is that why you turned on me every chance you could?"

"I couldn't help it," she wailed. "I had to blame you, to hate you, or…."

Or blame and hate yourself, Reeve thought as the woman trailed off into frenzied sobs.

She looked at Zach, assessing. She knew him

well enough to gauge his mood, knew that the taut lines of his tall body and the fierceness of his clenched fists were in reaction to roiled emotions, not aggressiveness. However much he might want to, Zach would not destroy with his own hands the woman who had brought this down on them.

He looked at Reeve then. "You were right," he said. "It would be a mercy she doesn't deserve."

Once she knew he was going to be all right, the investigator in Reeve took over. She knelt before Deborah, and with tremendous effort, was gentle with the woman.

"Deborah, listen to me. We still have to find him. Do you know where he went?"

She had to repeat the question twice more before it got through.

"No," she said. "No, he just was gone. Left me, just like that."

And came back months later to grab the child you'd allowed to grow to trust him, making it easy for him.

Reeve shook off the thought, knowing anger wasn't going to get her any answers.

"Did you and he ever talk about where you'd go?"

She was met with more crying.

Reeve moved closer, spoke softly, hoping natural instinct would make the woman quiet down so she could hear.

"It's the only way to redeem yourself now, Deborah. Help us catch him. Where might he go?"

Deborah gulped, making at least an effort to interrupt the weeping. "I…don't know."

"Did he ever talk about a place he liked to go, that he always went back to?"

"I…he said…there was a place in the mountains. His father built it. He liked to go back there to visit."

"Where? What mountains."

"I'm not sure, exactly. Here in California, though. He went once, right before….he left."

"Did he fly?"

Her forehead creased; at least she was thinking now. "No. I asked him if he wanted a ride to the airport, but he said it was only a few hours' drive."

"Do you know what route he was taking?"

"No."

"Did he say anything else about what he was going to do there?"

"Fishing. He said something about fishing. I remember that seemed odd because he was so…fastidious, I couldn't picture him dealing with worms and fish."

Reeve glanced up at Zach. "That should be enough. Between Draven and St. John, they'll find the cabin. They'll find him."

Zach nodded. His expression was unreadable, but the tension was still there in his body language.

"You'd better call them," he said.

"Yes."

She looked at Deborah, who had broken down once more. Her brain was saying leave her to her well-deserved pain, but her heart wouldn't let her just walk away from a woman so close to the edge.

She put a gentle hand on Deborah's knee. "Is there someone I can call for you? To be with you?"

"My…my sister."

It took Reeve a few minutes to get the number and make the call. Once she had assurances the sister would come immediately, she urged Zach out the door.

He didn't seem angry, not anymore. She wondered if the anger had been seared away by the bitter shock of why it had all happened. She couldn't imagine how he felt right now.

"I know you hate her, but I couldn't just leave her like that," she said when they were back in the elevator, feeling the need to explain.

He shrugged. "I hate what she did. But so does she, now, and she's going to punish herself more than I ever could."

"Yes," Reeve said, able to feel sorry for Deborah now that she knew the real reason behind her treatment of Zach.

He ran a hand through his hair, and Reeve saw how tired he suddenly looked. "I'm just glad to know. Finally." He gave her a look that warmed her to her soul. "Thank you for that."

Reeve reached over and hit the stop button on the elevator panel. They jolted to a halt. Zach looked at her as if he'd be curious if he had the energy.

"You," she said softly, "are quite something, Zachary Westin."

And then she put her arms around him, hugging him. She felt the tension in him as if it were a tangible thing, hard and wire-strung. And then she felt him shudder, as if it had all let go at once. And his arms came around her in turn as he almost sagged against her.

She tightened her hold on him, as if she could feed him strength through the fastness of her grip.

"You're quite something yourself," he whispered against her hair.

And Reeve had the crazy thought that she could stay here in this little box forever quite happily if it meant they could hang on to this.

Chapter 17

It was nice, Zach thought sleepily, to wake up in a home instead of a sterile, expressionless apartment. It was wonderful not to wake up to nightmares every day, but to actually look forward to the day not just with determination but with…anticipation? Excitement? Happiness?

That was a word he'd thought would never again be applied to himself. But it fit, now. And that was thanks to the best thing of all he woke up to these days. Reeve.

In the weeks since they'd confronted Deborah, his life had changed radically. It really had made a difference to know. Oh, he couldn't deny that the knowledge that the monster was still on the loose didn't hang over him like a dark cloud, ever threatening a storm of destruction, but he knew the police—Detective Tigard's fire rekindled when they'd plopped the answer on his desk—and Redstone's best were working on it, and if it could be done, they'd do it.

He'd felt a spark of guilt the first time he'd awakened and his first thought had been not of Scotty but of Reeve, warm and soft beside him, her body as sated as his after a night spent exploring just how high they could go. But then a memory had popped into his head, of the time when he'd discovered that, although he'd always been eager to go with his father when he suggested it, Scotty really didn't like swimming. Zach had asked him why he always said he wanted to go, and with the sometimes frightening wisdom of a child, the boy had said, "Because it makes you happy, Daddy. I like it when you're happy."

I like it when you're happy.

"You'd like it now, then, tiger," Zach whispered.

"You're smiling," Reeve said, startling him; he hadn't realized she was awake.

"Yes," he agreed.

He'd tell her, later. She'd understand what it all meant, the importance of it. She always did. But in the meantime, she was looking at him with those eyes, her hair tousled, her lips still looking thoroughly kissed...

But not kissed enough. Not nearly enough. He didn't know if he could ever kiss her lips—and every other part of her—enough.

But he was sure willing to give it a shot.

He'd gotten a good way toward that goal when Reeve asked, with that polite urgency that somehow drove him to the brink, if he would please stop driving her insane. Moments later, buried inside her and with her breasts filling his hands, it was he who was going insane, wildly insane with the sensations that flooded him. The soft curves of her, the feel of her mouth on him wherever she could reach, her fingers digging into his back as her hips rose to take him to the hilt, the searing, mind-stealing feel of her wet heat surrounding him, holding him, anchoring him.

She set the rhythm with the arching of her body, and he barely knew the groan of pleasure he heard each time she took him home was coming from his throat.

He'd thought the first time that his haste had been simply having gone without for so long. But now he knew it was Reeve, and that it was something he'd have to fight every time. But it was worth it, that battle to hold back, because now, when she shattered in his arms, when she cried out his name as her body clenched tightly around his, when he could finally let himself go, it was like nothing he'd ever felt or expected to feel in his life.

"Well," she said much later, when they were both breathing normally again, "good morning to you, too."

"Yes," he said simply.

She smiled then, understanding how momentous that simple word was. They stayed there for a few minutes longer, savoring the togetherness, before she reluctantly sat up.

"Caffeine," she said ruefully. "I'm going to need caffeine."

"I'll start the coffee while you shower," he said.

"Join me when you're done?" she asked.

"Oh, yes." Those lips needed kissing once more, he thought, and did it.

He made himself head out to the kitchen before he changed his mind and they never made it out of her bedroom. He was sleepily pouring the water into the well of the coffeemaker when he heard the sound from her office of the fax starting up. Knowing the thing sometimes spat the documents onto the floor, once the coffee was dripping he headed that way.

One of the two pages had indeed ended up on the floor. He picked it up, and reached for what looked to be the cover sheet out of the tray to put it in front.

And froze.

He stared down at the paper in his hand. Read the text. Read it again. Saw the signature. Knew it meant what he was reading was undeniably true.

He stood there for a long moment. A shudder ran through him. Instinctively he fought it down.

And then he began to move.

"Zach? What happened, I waited until I ran out of hot water…."

Reeve's voice trailed off as she reached the kitchen. The coffee was done, and it sat there, the carafe full, untouched.

"Zach?"

The call echoed back at her in that way that told her what she'd sensed on some level was true; the house was empty except for her.

He was gone.

She frowned. This was unlike him. She looked around, then spotted the paper on the table by the door where she left her keys and purse. His keys were gone.

Relieved that he'd at least left a note, she went over to get it. It was beyond terse, not even addressed to her by name.

Something came up. Talk to you later. Z.

"Well, fine," she muttered. Obviously flowery love notes aren't his style, she added to herself.

She poured herself a mug of coffee and took it with her back to the bedroom to sip while she finished drying her hair and getting dressed. When she was done she took the mug back to the kitchen, rinsed it and set it in the sink. Another yawn overtook her, and she knew she was going to be tired all day again.

Not, she thought with a fully pleasured smile curving her mouth, that it wasn't worth it. Her body was alive in places she hadn't even known existed. It was a new sensation for her, and she was savoring every moment of it.

She stretched, thought, then refilled the coffee mug and headed for her office to fire up her laptop and check mail. As she walked in, a patch of white snagged her peripheral vision, and she turned to look at the fax. A single page sat in the tray. She picked it up, puzzled when she saw it was a Redstone cover sheet. And only a cover sheet. The document it referred to wasn't there.

The fax must have screwed up, she thought.

The number on the cover sheet told her St. John had sent it, so when she opened her e-mail program she first looked for messages from him. She found only one. It was, as was all communication from St. John, short.

Found him. Info to follow via secure fax.

They'd found him. They'd found Scotty's murderer. Her heart began to race. She grabbed for the phone, the Redstone Security landline that Draven required them all to have for more secure communications. Her finger was on the speed dial button for St. John's office when it hit her.

Something came up....

A chill swept over her as the pieces fell together. The fax had worked just fine. But Zach had found it first. And now he was gone.

There was only one conclusion to draw.

Zach had gone after his son's killer.

Chapter 18

"He saw the fax before I did," Reeve said grimly.

She knew what she was telling them, admitting that Zach had been in her home this early in the morning. But it didn't matter now. What mattered now was finding him. Fast. Before he could do something they couldn't get him out of.

She'd called St. John first, to get the information he'd sent, that Zach had taken with him. And been at a loss for a moment when Josh answered, although it wasn't that unusual. He often answered St. John's line if the man himself was gone, just as he often answered his own in-house line, despite the fact that there probably wasn't another man on the planet at his level who would.

He told her Draven was there, in his office, about to follow up on the lead St. John had faxed her. She quickly decided it was just as well, it might take both of them to help her get Zach out of this.

"How long ago?" That was Draven.

"Probably as the fax came in." She almost added "I was in the shower," but that was more than she wanted to admit and reeked of giving an excuse so she didn't.

"He had transportation?"

"Yes. His own car."

"It'll take him a couple of hours to drive there and find the cabin at best," Draven said, "but he's got a half-hour headstart, minimum."

"There's an airport at the east end of the lake," Josh said. "Small, but I can get the Hawk III in there. I'll call ahead and have her ready, and we can be airborne in less than an hour. We'll get there right behind him."

For a moment Reeve couldn't speak. She loved this man. Darn near king of the world, and he never hesitated an instant if it was for one of his own.

"We'll meet at the airfield," Draven said.

"On my way," Reeve said.

She was closer, so she beat them to the back side of the county airport where Redstone Aviation's hangars were. The Hawk III was already out on the hangar apron, and she saw the fuel truck pulling away; when Josh Redstone spoke, things happened fast.

She drove past the open first hangar and back to the second one, which was where Redstone Security was headquartered. With all their gear here, it was convenient for quick departures when necessary. They had a communications center, a bunk room and a large, secured room they called the equipment locker that held everything from makeup for disguises to explosives. It was the perfect spot for them, spacious, well-equipped, and private; any Redstone personnel who came through used the other hangar nearer the airfield.

It felt odd to Reeve; she hadn't been here in quite some time. Yet it came back to her quickly under the pressure of the situation. She keyed in her code and stood for the retinal scan, and then she was in.

She went quickly to her locker to get a weapon; Schumer had no record of being armed, but she wanted to be ready for anything. She picked a small .38 that she could easily conceal, the weight of it comforting in her hand as she thought of the man who had butchered Zach's son.

She didn't want Zach to kill him, she thought, but she wouldn't have a qualm about doing it herself if she had to.

The flurry of familiar activity as they boarded and Josh took the pilot's seat was just the distraction she needed. She could feel Draven watching her; those alert eyes never missed a thing. He hadn't said anything out of the ordinary to her, but his mere presence always brought the very air around him to life. Marriage to Grace O'Conner might have mellowed him in some ways, but on the job he was the same Draven who had become legend.

"Where's Tess?" Reeve asked, inquiring about the woman who usually flew Josh these days, since he'd had to concede he couldn't fly and get done the work he needed to do at the same time.

"Visiting her sister," Josh said. "She just had a baby."

"Aunt Tess? Wonderful," Reeve said.

"She'll be good at it," Josh said. "Like she is at everything."

That she would, Reeve thought. Tess Machado had been with Redstone in one capacity or another for nearly ten years, and had proven herself while literally under fire. Reeve had come to know her a little during flights to various assignments, and she'd been impressed with her quiet intensity and intelligence as much as with her undoubted skill at the controls of anything that flew.

She watched Josh as he settled in at the controls. He acted as if it were nothing that he was here, doing this, when he had a multi-billion-dollar empire to run.

"Thank you," she said

Josh glanced up. "He's Redstone," he said simply. "If I can help, I will."

Reeve gave him a smile that she hoped told him

her feelings. "We'd all walk into hell for you. Maybe Zach will walk out."

Josh's eyes widened. Amazingly, he looked flustered. Or at the least embarrassed at her words.

"Good point," Draven said, adding to Josh's discomfiture.

Reeve made sure her voice was normal when she granted him a distraction.

"Have you been to this airport before?" she asked.

"Yes," Josh said, quickly enough to betray his relief; Josh didn't like his extraordinary behavior pointed out, because he didn't feel it was extraordinary. "Been a while since I landed at any mountain airport, though."

"Information or warning?" Draven asked, his tone dry.

"Both," Josh said with a chuckle. "It's an art. Winds can be tricky, so you don't try to set down on the numbers. Got to have an idea what the wind is doing down on the runway, so you go a bit further before you touch down."

"Hope it's a long runway," Draven said in the same tone.

"About a mile. It'll be close."

"Mr. Redstone?"

The young man in the gray-and-red jumpsuit who was charged with getting the plane ready stuck his head in the cockpit.

"Got the report." He handed Josh a printed page.

"Here's the radio frequencies. First one's weather, second is specialized wind reports. No NOTAMs. Clear, unlimited visibility, winds are steady at eleven miles per hour, no reports of shear."

Josh nodded. "Okay."

"Only thing is, the temp at the airfield now is fifty-five, expected to rise to near seventy by noon."

"We'd better get moving then," Josh said.

Reeve waited until the attendant had gone and Draven had pulled up the stairs and secured the door before asking, "What's a NOTAM? And why does the temperature matter so much?"

"Notice to airmen. And density altitude," Josh said as he set controls and pulled on the pilot's headset. "The airport's at almost seven thousand feet, so it's a factor. Cold air is dense, you get lift sooner. When the air's warm, the molecules expand so it's thinner. Landing's not so bad, but taking off and clearing trees and mountains can be an adventure."

"Oh."

"Sorry you asked?" Draven asked, the quirk of his mouth causing the scar along the left side of his face to tighten.

"Almost," she admitted.

They went back to the cabin to take seats and belt themselves in, and let Josh concentrate on the task of getting them airborne.

"He does love this, doesn't he?" Reeve said when they were settled.

"Josh is first and foremost a pilot," Draven agreed. "And I think he'd go back to being just a pilot who built the occasional plane in a minute."

They sat in silence during the smooth, perfect takeoff, and any concern she'd had after that talk of mountain airports eased; Josh had been flying most of his life, he could handle anything that happened.

She leaned back in her seat, a chair more comfortable than some living-room furniture she'd been in. They were up to the Hawk V now, but this plane was still top of the line. Smaller and able to land on shorter runways around the world, it was still in high demand. But any plane designed by Josh Redstone was always in high demand; his reputation as a designer and builder was unmatched, and hadn't been diluted much by the fact that he now led an empire that stretched literally around the world.

Finally, she couldn't distract herself any longer, and worry about Zach crept in and took over. She could only guess how he was feeling by imagining what she would do if suddenly handed the whereabouts of the person who had destroyed her life. And she had to admit, she'd probably be right where he was.

She understood. Completely. She just didn't want him to pay the price that would follow. He'd paid enough. Too much.

"He'll be all right, Reeve."

Her gaze shot to Draven, and she wondered what had shown in her face.

He smiled at her, a soft, rueful smile, and she wondered what was showing in her face now.

"It's still new to me," he said quietly. "So I'm more…aware of it in others. You love him, don't you."

His inflection made clear it wasn't really a question. And, she realized, he was right. It wasn't a question at all. She did love Zach. And judging by the fact that there was no jolt, no jump of shock, she apparently had for a long time.

"Yes." She heard herself say it, heard the lack of any doubt or hesitation in her voice, and marveled at it.

"Does he know?"

"I haven't said anything, if that's what you mean."

"Not necessarily," he said, an undertone in his voice that made her wonder when and how he'd realized he loved Grace too much to go on with his solitary life.

The sleek little jet made short work of the trip, and Josh made smooth work of the landing she'd been a little too aware of. Which was odd, because she'd certainly flown into tighter, smaller places, with much less to recommend them as far as finished air-fields go. It had to be that she was worried about Zach, and it was spilling over, she thought as they taxied over to the parking area alongside the runway.

"We were lucky the wind didn't pick up," Josh

said as he pulled off the headset. "Those noise-abatement regs can make things difficult."

Reeve exchanged a glance with Draven, and they both suppressed a smile. The convoluted problems of Redstone must make the complex but straightforward problems of flying seem a relief for him.

"Come on," Josh said once they were out on the ground, and started walking away from the small terminal building and toward the rows of hangars strung out along the runway. "Buddy of mine runs a detailing operation here. We're borrowing a vehicle from him."

Again Reeve suppressed a smile; Josh, she had learned early on, had friends everywhere. He'd done a lot of wandering in the early days, and she knew the friends he'd made then were the ones he treasured most now, because they'd become friends when he was just that tall, lanky kid with the drawl and a dream, not the head of an empire.

George Callahan greeted Josh with a grin and a bear hug. He also understood when Josh said the niceties would have to wait until they got back, and handed over a set of keys and pointed them at a fairly new four-wheel-drive crew cab pickup with Callahan Aviation Services painted on the door.

"I flew, you drive," Josh said and handed the keys to Draven before climbing into the back seat. He looked at Reeve. "And you, just hang on until we find him."

Reeve didn't have to ask what he meant; catching the killer would be a side benefit, but taking care of his own always came first with Josh.

The map Draven had printed out and brought was accurate, and they easily found the cabin Schumer's parents had bought decades ago. Reeve felt a quiver of dread when she saw Zach's car parked at a haphazard angle in the gravel road in front of the cabin. She leapt out and ran to it.

"Hot," she reported. They were literally right behind him.

There was another car in the driveway, and Draven pulled in behind it, effectively blocking escape. A split second after he'd opened his door, she heard a crash from inside the cabin.

She and Draven reacted in the same instant.

"I'll take the back," Draven said and was gone at a low, crouching run.

Reeve never stopped moving, just acknowledged his words and kept going, drawing her weapon as she went. Neither of them worried about Josh; a large part of his success lay in his understanding that when you hire the best, you should let them do what they do best, which usually meant you stayed out of their way.

The front door was closed, but not locked. For a brief moment she contemplated knocking, but she didn't want to tip off Schumer if Zach was in trouble. He was good at what he did, but he wasn't trained the way Redstone Security was. She wanted to know what the situation was first.

She eased the door open until she could see part of the main room of the cabin. A kitchen setup lined one end wall, and a large fireplace the other. A hallway split the back wall, and the two doors she saw, one open and one closed, told her they probably led to a bathroom and a bedroom.

A shout came from that direction. The words were muffled, but she knew it wasn't Zach's voice.

"Please," she breathed as she moved with silent speed to the closed door. She heard movement inside. Then a heavy thud. She couldn't wait. Zach was in there with a desperate, cornered killer who had nothing to lose. She settled her grip on the .38. She saw movement from the corner of her eye and knew Draven was coming in from the back. She also knew he'd read the situation and would be at her back.

She threw open the door.

"Thank God!" The man in the corner called out to them gratefully. "Are you the cops? Get this crazy—"

His words degenerated into a choking gasp. He was in the corner because he'd been backed there by the man who now had his hands on his throat.

Zach.

Schumer was turning red in the face. His hands were flailing. Clawing at Zach. Zach never flinched. He kept his hold.

"Zach," Reeve said. "Stop."

He either couldn't or chose not to hear her.

"He deserves it, Zach. But not yet. Let go."

Zach only tightened his grip. Schumer kicked at him, but weakly.

"Zach, we need him. Do you really think Scotty was the first? Or even the last? There are others, Zach, there have to be. Other victims. We need this pervert alive to find them."

For the first time, he seemed to waver. "He's already picked out his next ones," he said hoarsely. "He's working on a woman here, with two little boys."

"You're crazy," Schumer squeaked out. "I never—" He gagged as Zach tightened his grip once more.

"You never will again," Zach said.

Reeve stood there, aching inside because she understood so well how he felt, and it would give her no small amount of satisfaction herself if she ended up looking at this piece of human refuse dead at her feet.

But not by Zach's hand. She knew what it would mean, what he would have to go through, that he'd have to relive every second of his son's kidnapping and awful death all over again, even if they didn't press murder charges against him. And she knew that, however justified it might be, that it would change him, that he would not shrug it off and go on, that it would in some way haunt him.

"Zach," she said softly.

Draven was there, gun drawn, waiting, letting her take the lead. She heard new footsteps approaching, and knew that Josh was there as well. She put her weapon back in the holster at the small of her back. She reached out and touched him, put a hand gently but firmly on his arm.

"Zach, don't. You don't want to go through what this would cause."

"I don't care."

"I know," she said, her voice tight with emotion she didn't try to hide. "But I do."

She felt a shudder go through him.

"I care, Zach. I love you. And I don't want to lose you, and what we have, what we can have, because of that piece of scum."

He went still. For a long, silent moment he didn't move. Then, slowly, he turned his head to look at her. He relaxed his grip, and Schumer slid down the wall into a weeping huddle on the floor.

"Reeve?" Zach whispered.

"Please, Zach." She tightened her grip on his arm, and laid her other hand on his back. "Don't risk us for him."

He turned then. She was aware of Draven moving, grabbing Schumer and yanking him to his feet. The man was blubbering unintelligibly as Draven dragged him out of the room. Josh, who had apparently been standing just outside, appeared in the doorway.

As she turned back to Zach, Reeve heard a cell phone ring, but she ignored it and kept her eyes on Zach's face, trying to read him. She heard Josh answer as if it were from a distance. He listened for a moment, then said goodbye and disconnected.

"Reeve?" He said it gently, as if he felt he was intruding. She turned her head to look at him. "That was St. John. He's been continuing to probe. He's found at least four other cases."

Zach made a sound, low and harsh. "All dead?" he asked.

"Yes," Josh said reluctantly. "And all the same method. It's how he stayed out of the system. He picked his victim, charmed the mother, learned what he needed to know, then left. And came back after he figured he'd been forgotten."

"And counted on the woman's silence about her affair," Reeve said.

Zach's eyes closed, and the pain on his face was too much for Reeve to bear. She reached for him. He came into her arms, a low, exhausted sound breaking from him.

"I can see it wasn't me he needed," Josh said, and when Reeve glanced at him, he smiled in understanding. "We'll be outside."

She held Zach, tightening her grasp, knowing that at times like this you were half-numb, and it took more to register.

"It's done, Zach. You got him."

"But it's not over. There'll be a trial, it'll all come out again…"

"Better him on trial than you," she said, and hugged him tighter. "Besides, the life expectancy of child molesters in prison is often measured in days, not years. And Draven knows people who can…hurry that along."

She felt no qualms about that. The man who had raped, tortured and murdered Scott Westin had surrendered his right to human feeling long ago.

Zach didn't say anything for a long time. Reeve didn't care, she just wanted to hold him, to feel his arms around her in turn.

Then, finally, he asked, "Did you mean it?"

She was too honest to pretend she didn't know what he meant. "Yes. I did. But it's all right, Zach, I understand that—"

"I love you, too."

She froze.

"I didn't think I could. Ever would. I didn't think there was any way out of this nightmare. But you… you led me home, Reeve. Made me feel something besides pain and…ice."

She breathed out his name.

Zach shivered, tightened his hold.

Peace at last.

Epilogue

"Another wedding?"

Draven turned his attention from the sheriff who was loading Schumer into the back of his unit to his boss.

"Looks that way," he said.

Josh shook his head in wonder. "Amazing. It's like it's in the air. When St. John tells me he's getting married, then I'll know the world's coming to an end."

Draven watched Josh go over to shake hands with the deputy, who would probably be talking for months about how he'd met one of the most famous men in the world.

It's not only St. John I'd like to see find happiness again, Draven thought.

He heard a sound and looked back at the cabin as Zach and Reeve came out. As he saw what was so clear in their faces, he made a silent wish that the Redstone magic would work someday for the man who most deserved it.

He grinned inwardly at himself, and then touched the ring on his left hand, put there by the woman who had turned him into a mooning romantic.

It was definitely in the air.

* * * * *

Silhouette® Romantic Suspense
keeps getting hotter!

Turn the page for a sneak preview of
New York Times *bestselling author*
Beverly Barton's latest title from
THE PROTECTORS *miniseries.*

HIS ONLY OBSESSION
by Beverly Barton

On sale March 2007
wherever books are sold.

Gwen took a taxi to the Yellow Parrot, and with each passing block she grew more tense. It didn't take a rocket scientist to figure out that this dive was in the worst part of town. Gwen had learned to take care of herself, but the minute she entered the bar, she realized that a smart woman would have brought a gun with her. The interior was hot, smelly and dirty, and the air was so smoky that it looked as if a pea soup fog had settled inside the building. Before she had gone three feet, an old drunk came up to her and asked for money. Side-stepping him, she searched for someone who looked as if he or she might actually work here, someone other than the prostitutes who were trolling for customers.

After fending off a couple of grasping young men and ignoring several vulgar propositions in an odd mixture of Spanish and English, Gwen found the bar. She ordered a beer from the burly, bearded bartender. When he set the beer in front of her, she took the opportunity to speak to him.

"I'm looking for a man. An older American man, in his seventies. He was probably with a younger woman. This man is my father and—"

"*No hablo inglés*."

"Oh." He didn't speak English and she didn't speak Spanish. Now what?

While she was considering her options, Gwen noticed a young man in skintight black pants and an open black shirt, easing closer and closer to her as he made his way past the other men at the bar.

Great. That was all she needed—some horny young guy mistaking her for a prostitute.

"*Señorita*." His voice was softly accented and slightly slurred. His breath smelled of liquor. "You are all alone, *sí?*"

"Please, go away," Gwen said. "I'm not interested."

He laughed, as if he found her attitude amusing. "Then it is for me to make you interested. I am Marco. And you are…?"

"Leaving," Gwen said.

She realized it had been a mistake to come here

alone tonight. Any effort to unearth information about her father in a place like this was probably pointless. She would do better to come back tomorrow and try to speak to the owner. But when she tried to move past her ardent young suitor, he reached out and grabbed her arm. She tensed.

Looking him right in the eyes, she told him, "Let go of me. Right now."

"But you cannot leave. The night is young."

Gwen tugged on her arm, trying to break free. He tightened his hold, his fingers biting into her flesh. With her heart beating rapidly as her basic fight-or-flight instinct kicked in, she glared at the man.

"I'm going to ask you one more time to let me go."

Grinning smugly, he grabbed her other arm, holding her in place.

Suddenly, seemingly from out of nowhere, a big hand clamped down on Marco's shoulder, jerked him back and spun him around. Suddenly free, Gwen swayed slightly but managed to retain her balance as she watched in amazement as a tall, lanky man in jeans and cowboy boots shoved her would-be suitor up against the bar.

"I believe the lady asked you real nice to let her go," the man said in a deep Texas drawl. "Where I come from, a gentleman respects a lady's wishes."

Marco grumbled something unintelligible in Spanish. Probably cursing, Gwen thought. Or maybe praying. If she were Marco, she would be praying that the big, rugged American wouldn't beat her to a pulp.

Apparently Marco was not as smart as she was. When the Texan released him, he came at her rescuer, obviously intending to fight him. The Texan took Marco out with two swift punches, sending the younger man to the floor. Gwen glanced down at where Marco lay sprawled flat on his back, unconscious.

Her hero turned to her. "Ma'am, are you all right?"

She nodded. The man was about six-two, with a sunburned tan, sun-streaked brown hair and azure-blue eyes.

"What's a lady like you doing in a place like this?" he asked.

This February...

Catch NASCAR Superstar **Carl Edwards** *in*

SPEED DATING!

Kendall assesses risk for a living—so she's the last person you'd expect to see on the arm of a race-car driver who thrives on the unpredictable. But when a bizarre turn of events—and NASCAR hotshot Dylan Hargreave—inspire her to trade in her ever-so-structured existence for "life in the fast lane" she starts to feel she might be on to something!

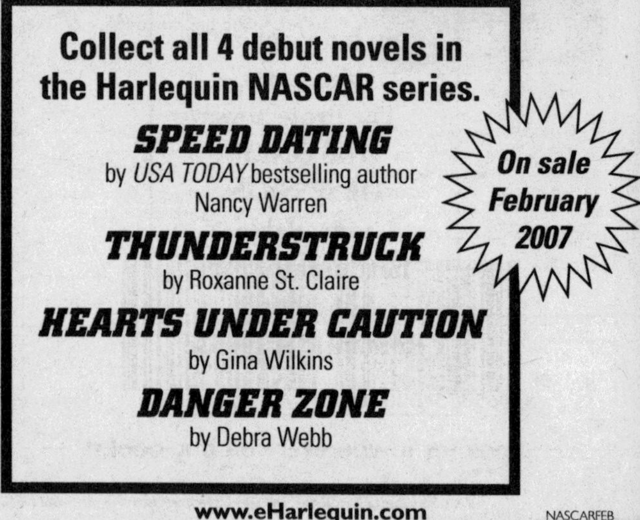

www.eHarlequin.com

NASCARFEB

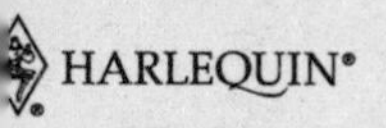

EVERLASTING LOVE™

Every great love has a story to tell™

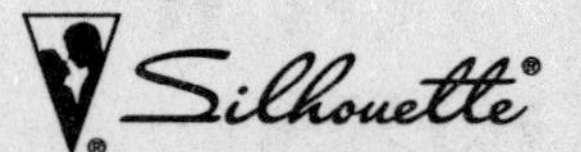

Romantic

SUSPENSE

COMING NEXT MONTH

#1455 HIS ONLY OBSESSION—Beverly Barton
The Protectors
After rescuing the alluring Dr. Gwen Arnell, Dundee agent Will Pierce realizes that they are both searching for the same man. Together they set sail, island-hopping in their quest to find their target and a mysterious youth serum…while battling an attraction neither can deny.

#1456 MISSION: M.D.—Linda Turner
Turning Points
Rachel Martin is dying to seduce the gorgeous doctor who lives next door, but a stalker wants to stop her. Will Rachel be able to keep her distance despite the growing desire she feels for her neighbor?

#1457 SHADOW SURRENDER—Linda Conrad
Night Guardians
Special Agent Teal Benaly finds dangers hidden at every turn as she sets out to investigate a strange murder on the Navajo reservation. But nothing holds the potential danger she finds in the arms of the dark stranger sent to protect her.

#1458 ONE HOT TARGET—Diane Pershing
When an innocent woman dies, police believe that Carmen Coyle might have been the potential target. With the help of her lawyer-friend JR Ellis, Carmen tries to track down possible leads—and resist the temptation to explore a more personal relationship with JR.

SRSCNM0207